# *The Uncertainty Principle*

MACMILLAN'S
*Best of Soviet Science Fiction*

Arkady and Boris Strugatsky
*Roadside Picnic and Tale of the Troika*
*Prisoners of Power*
*Definitely Maybe*
*Noon: 22nd Century*
*Far Rainbow/The Second Invasion from Mars*
*The Ugly Swans*

Kirill Bulychev
*Half a Life*

Mikhail Emtsev and Eremei Parnov
*World Soul*

Dmitri Bilenkin
*The Uncertainty Principle*

Vladimir Savchenko
*Self-Discovery*

# The Uncertainty Principle

## DMITRI BILENKIN

TRANSLATED FROM THE RUSSIAN BY *Antonina W. Bouis*

INTRODUCTION BY *Theodore Sturgeon*

COLLIER BOOKS
*A Division of Macmillan Publishing Co., Inc.*
*New York*
COLLIER MACMILLAN PUBLISHERS
*London*

Macmillan Publishing Co., Inc.
866 Third Avenue, New York, N.Y. 10022
Collier Macmillan Canada, Ltd.

Library of Congress Cataloging in Publication Data
Bilenkin, Dmitrii Aleksandrovich.
The uncertainty principle.
Selection of the author's short stories.
I. Title.
PZ4.B5965Un [PG3479.4.I4] 891.7'3'44
ISBN 0-02-510770-4 78-9620
ISBN 0-02-016600-1 pbk

*The Uncertainty Principle* is also published in a hardcover edition by Macmillan Publishing Co., Inc.

First Collier Books Edition 1979
Printed in the United States of America

# Contents

# Introduction

Beginning in 1939, the late, great science fiction editor John W. Campbell gathered about him, in a mere eighteen months, a stable of writers who since have become monuments in the genre: Asimov, Heinlein, de Camp, del Rey, Simak, Clark, Hubbard (who deserted the field to found Dianetics and Scientology, but who was one of the big ones while he lasted), and many others.

If I ever perfect my time machine, I shall go to the Soviet Union, snatch up Dmitri Bilenkin, whisk him back to 1939, take him to the creaky old building at 79 Seventh Avenue, lead him through the maze formed by high stacks of magazines and huge rolls of virgin paper (the aroma of which clings to me to this day) to the small office barely containing the big man sitting there: "John," I will say, "John—here's another one for you."

Bilenkin evokes this adventure for a number of reasons. He is, as you will discover, fascinated by the idea of time travel—the paradoxes confronted, the ethical questions involved in altering the past even by the fall of an eyelash—and by the possibility that such wounds in time may, after all, be self-healing.

He is also a fantasist—not your run-of-the-rune-dragon-and-goblin fantasist, but the creator of what Campbell called "wacky" fantasy. Coupling outrageous concepts with a wild sense of humor is no small feat, but Bilenkin has mastered it, as you will see in the tale of the professor on the bicycle who meets an unfortunate citizen floating in midair, begging to be brought down, and in the saga of the haunted spaceship. John Campbell had two magazines—*Astounding* (later, *Analog*) and *Unknown.* Not all of his "golden age" authors could write for both. Without question, Bilenkin could have.

One other way in which Bilenkov has a Campbellian flavor is in his social concerns, and in his handling of them. Isaac Asimov once wrote that science fiction contains three elements (often stirring all three into the same story in varying amounts): "What if . . . ," "If only . . . ," and "If this goes on . . . ," and it is this latter which makes for the most interesting sociological science fiction. Bilenkin gives us, for example, a computer which can take a young person's personality profile and academic record and announce whether or not that person's goal in life is realistic; if not, it suggests alternative pursuits better matched to his talents. Good idea? you might ask. Save a lot of waste motion, a lot of heartache? And in comes a young man who wants to be a poet—burns to be a poet. The computer flips out a card which says he will not be. Anguished, the youngster crumples up the card and flings it out of the window. (Lovely touch: the card refuses to be wrinkled, straightens out its plastic surfaces and flutters to the ground undamaged.) The professor, who is also the inventor of this technique, pauses for a moment to wonder if, after all, he is doing the right thing, and then he—but no, I won't tell you; read it for yourself.

Bilenkin is touched, reached by beauty; beauty is the subject of another solid science fiction about a sun in a distant galaxy which must, for the good of humanity, be destroyed, and with it, a planet of ice, a world of almost indescribable beauty. Here the technological imperative is in direct confrontation with the esthetic, and it is in the hands of the members of the expedition to make the choice. And unlike so many other narratives, this is by no means a life-and-death choice, and these people will have to live with the consequences of their decision.

These ethical concerns are central to many of Bilenkin's stories. What if, despite rigorous and meticulous safeguards against interference with an intelligent species, we do irreversible damage to one—not by landing on a planet, but merely by examining it? What is our responsibility if, on discovering the grave of a world-shaking, historical barbarian, we isolate his cell pattern and graft it to an infant, bringing him up in modern society? What is the moral position of a truly great scientific theoretician who uses his almost-legendary reputation to suppress his greatest discovery? What *really* is the motivation of men who pit muscle against mountain (profoundly explored in one of the finest stories in this book; the mountain is Olympus, the largest and most magnificent in our solar system, and it is on Mars)? Is it right to slaughter and slaughter and slaughter charging herbivores without knowing why they are charging? (There have been few fables like this one since Androcles understood that the lion roared, not in anger, but in agony.)

Bilenkin is by no means an antiscience science fiction writer. (There are such.) Underlying his world-view is, along with a profound respect for the potentialities of science and its ability to open doors to achievement and to understanding both outer space and that far more vast inner space of the mind and heart, the fact—forgotten by so many science-worshippers—that respected and orthodox science gave us leeches and cups to draw blood from the desperately ill, malformed babies, filthy air, denuded hillsides, dead lakes, and industrial disasters. Nowhere is this more poignantly presented than in the story of the fine artist who has located one of the very few untouched natural areas left in his near-future world, and settles in to paint it. (Here again Bilenkin's rich and delicate appreciation for nuances of color and texture is beautifully exercised.) The intrusion of technology at this point is utterly inexcusable, for all its neat logic, but what makes the point so sharply is that it is ludicrous. That the painter's sensibilities should be so shattered is of course tragic; but that it should have been done so *stupidly*!

I think—and this is a truly subjective opinion—that of all items on this writer's wide spectrum, I enjoy most what I have called his *Unknown* stories—for example, the one about the bank teller who hears a news report from *tomorrow* that his bank has been robbed, and how he lives through the next day trying to make it not happen; O. Henry himself would have wished his by-line on this one. And—would you believe it?—a deal-with-the-devil story with a genuinely original twist; didn't you think they had all been used up by now? And the havoc caused by the invention of a Time Bank, into which you could deposit time spent uselessly, and withdraw it when you wanted to keep on doing something you otherwise hadn't time for.

Campbell's *Unknown*, however, had a different kind of fantasy beside the "wacky" and hilarious: the very essence of Asimov's "What if . . . ?" applied to intensely human, deeply moving situations and predicaments. Here is an old man, poverty-stricken and dying, who has a special talent. By his presence with creative people, he is a catalyst for their creativity. They are hardly, or not at all, aware of his presence, but through it they build great structures, write great literature. He is unacknowledged and unrewarded for this, and few have ever known he was alive; none mourns his death. And why did he so urgently seek out people in the act of creation? Because it warmed him—that's all. Because it warmed him.

Science fiction defies exact definition, and probably always will, which does not deter the tireless efforts of writers, readers, and educators to draw a distinction between science fiction and fantasy. John Campbell came close to a pragmatic distinction when, in a directive to his authors, he said, "For *Astounding* I want stories that are logical, possible, and good. For *Unknown* I want stories that are logical and good."

I don't know in what cubbyhole the taxonomists will place Dmitri Bilenkin, but they will not dilute this one unassailable dictum: He is good.

—Theodore Sturgeon
San Diego, 1978

# The Uncertainty Principle

# *The Uncertainty Principle*

"In traveling to the past, you can either appear in a predetermined point in space or in a predetermined point in time. In principle, it is impossible to do both simultaneously."

(*Fundamental Temporalics,* A.D. 2023)

HIS FEET SLIPPED often, and this worried Berg. He was used to mud-proof footwear, and was suspiciously clumsy in the rough, badly fitting boots when the mud stuck to them in a gloppy clump. And it kept happening on this washed-out road. A minor point, which they had overlooked. How many others would he discover?

Luckily, the road was deserted.

The clay changed to sand, and Berg sighed in relief. He stopped on a hilltop. A lone oak was shedding leaves, which gently glided down to earth. The fields were mown and stretched out in a gray haze on the horizon, and the sky, like the earth, was gloomy and dark. Far ahead, where the road led, he could barely make out the spire of a country church. The rain obscured the view.

The planners hadn't let him down—this was the place. But the time? What century had the principle of temporal uncertainty thrown him into? The seventh, the seventeenth? It looked as if he'd have to wait until he got into town to find out.

Only now, as he strode along the wet sand, did Berg sense the difference between the air of this period that he had come to and that of the time he had left. A twentieth-century man would have experienced an easily explained difference: the cleanliness of the present atmosphere. But for Berg and his time the years were long gone when, say, the factory exhausts of North America polluted the air in Hawaii. What was the difference, then? Perhaps the air from Berg's time was permanently marked by the technosphere, with its embryomachines, oxidan, and synthetics. That must be it. Here, in this century, the smells of the forests, earth, and grasses were obviously lacking something. Something . . .

"And the skies of the centuries are as unique as the days of our lives." He thought of Sheer's poem.

And the skies of the centuries are unique.

There was no need to hurry, since he should enter the town at dusk. His clothes were carefully copied from the outfit of an itinerant tinker, but the trouble was that they might not fit the century he had landed in. Of course, the clothes of medieval tinkers were not sensitive to the latest changes in fashion, and most important, he would be a foreigner to them, and therefore entitled to wear unusual clothes. After all, this was the first—and, let's hope, the last—trip by man into the past.

Here he was in a world that had been dead for centuries. Soon he would see his ancient ancestors, whose bones had turned to dust long ago. And now they were strolling along the streets, sitting in taverns, loving, arguing, laughing.

It was crazy, unbelievable, but true. But if you think about it, the future is much more unreal for the past than the past is for the future. Because the past has existed. And the future is nothing, a void, mere white mist. Berg would be a visitor from somewhere that did not exist for anyone he met. Amusing. Berg looked at his hands. Normal, strong, callused hands. Berg chuckled, remembering the scientific council and their debate on how best to reproduce the medieval calluses.

The road led to the village, but Berg took a side path that went through the forest and around the settlement. He was not afraid of premature questions and meetings, but knew that the services of a tinker might be in demand in the village, and delays were not part of his plan.

The forest had little resemblance to the neat woodlands of his own time. Underbrush, broken branches, thickets—it was almost impenetrable. It spoke of no people, of a lack of manpower, of the self-contained isolation of the villages. The high road was a narrow strip of mud, last used by a wagon before the rain. The path was made by animals, even though the village was nearby. It looked as if he had landed in the early Middle Ages. Maybe too early?

There was a pine grove on the other side of a dark ravine, and he caught a glimpse of the church through the clearing on the right, and then the trees blocked the view once more. A flock of crows cawed above him. Rain fell from the darkened sky. Red and white mushrooms dotted the ground under the pines. Soon he came upon grass-covered mounds and gray, listing crosses. A cemetery. He could make out some of the inscriptions. He read dates, worn biblical passages: words of sorrow and grief.

Suddenly his heart skipped a beat. There in the bushes was a new white cross, and the name on it was Berg.

The grave was so fresh that the clay was still dry. A shiver went through Berg: he was going to be killed here, in this time, and they would bury him.

He barely managed to still his thumping heart. What nonsense! The man they buried was dead, and he was alive! And there was no mystery here. A coincidence. Berg was a common name. There must be dozens of generations of MacPhersons in Scotland. Maybe the Berg family name is just as old, and some of them lived here. But that meant . . . that meant, that he might meet . . . of course, hadn't he known that before?

Quickly leaving the grave, Berg shook his head. It was simple math and nothing more. Everyone has two parents, four grandparents, eight great-grandparents, sixteen great-great-grandparents, and going back ten generations, more than a thousand ancestors, and if you go way back . . . Even taking distant cousins marrying into account, even so, probably most of the inhabitants of any European settlement had a direct relationship with Berg of the twenty-first century. And some Caesar Gaius or other he could treat as a close relative.

What a frightening thing heredity was.

No matter how he tried to calm himself, the incident left an unpleasant taste in his mouth. He walked faster to get out of the cemetery. Just think: every twentieth (tenth, seventh) person buried here was a direct ancestor of his! Berg was sickened at the thought that his appearance, personality, and very existence hung on such a slender thread. If someone in the Middle Ages had not met someone else or had had a fight, maybe right in the very city he was visiting, then maybe Berg would not exist! Or he would have different-colored eyes and a different personality, a different destiny.

And that was one of the reasons no one had been given permission to visit the past.

Berg calmed down only when the path led out onto the road with its hills and distant vistas.

A breeze sprang up. A murky, narrow river appeared around a bend, with a dirty bridge leading to rather unimposing fortress gates. Berg stopped, quickly checking the jagged silhouette of the city walls. There it was! He quickly found the profile of the Fat Maiden, familiar from photographs. That meant he was in luck, he had ended up in approximately the right period, because the tower had not been built before the tenth century and had been destroyed in the fourteenth by the knights of the Duke of Berkeley. That also meant that his costume would do, and he didn't have to change in the bushes.

He took out the spare costumes and poured a liquid on them that resembled wine in taste and color. When he was satisfied that the cloth had turned to dust, he headed toward the bridge.

His mind was cool and clear as he stepped onto the bridge, and irrelevant thoughts disappeared. And yet it seemed to him that all he had to do was shake his head and it would all be gone.

But no, the dogs that attacked him as he crossed the bridge were all too real. There was a pack of them—dirty, mangy, ragged. Crouching close to the ground, they barked at him angrily.

"What's this?" Berg thought, holding his staff tighter. "I haven't the slightest idea what a traveler does when he meets up with a pack of . . . and what's the matter with them, anyway?"

The dogs backed away when he took a step toward them. The growling was replaced with confused whining, which contained both hostility and fear. Berg suddenly understood. Of course! His clothes and shoes still had the smell of the time in which they were made—the strange foreign smell of synthetics!

Berg looked at the dogs with new respect, then, paying them no attention, moved toward the gates. The most important moment was coming up, the moment that would decide the effectiveness of his masquerade.

But nothing happened. A face looked out from a barred window and disappeared. He could hear dice clicking in the guard's booth—they obviously weren't about to interrupt an exciting game for some beggar.

"It looks as though I've come in time of peace," Berg decided.

Man was forbidden from visiting the past, but there was nothing wrong with sending chronoscopes, disguised as clouds, to photograph and observe the past. Of course, because of the uncertainty principle they had to be sent out rather haphazardly. If it was just a question of going back a few years, then the location could be pretty well controlled, but even a few years more made the results totally unpredictable. There was just no way to send a computer to the battlefield of Cressy. Of course, the equipment could be set for the exact time of the battle, but in that case the camera would appear anywhere but over the village of Cressy. Or, conversely, the camera could be stationed directly over the battle site, but no one could predict by how many centuries or millennia it would be off.

That wasn't too much of a problem, because historians were interested in all eras. Most often, the cameras were sent to specific places, resulting in very disjointed time continuity. But it was better than nothing. Everything went well, until the accident. A cumulus-cloud camera did not respond to the return command. So they plotted its course to collide with a storm cloud, where the steady lightning bolts would mark the explosion. But the destruct mechanism failed too. The crystal bloc of the nonlinear antigravitator survived, in a damaged condition. And to compound the problems, it happened not far from a town.

Thus, a product of the twenty-first century appeared in the eleventh, and quite possibly, fell into the hands of people. Of course, the molten "rock" should not have created any suspicions. But the crystal might survive the wars, fires, and uprisings, and slip into the twentieth century, where its synthetic nature would certainly be recognized. A premature discovery, a dangerous one that could alter the course of history—that's all they needed.

The crowded streets did not impress Berg—he had studied them carefully. But the smells, the stench of garbage, horse manure, and something worse than that. "Slow down," Berg told himself. "A thousand years ago, people didn't hurry so much." Hiking up his cassock, a priest stepped over a puddle. Another howling dog challenged him, then retreated.

It was getting dark, but his appearance did not go unnoticed: the few passersby looked him over. Not for any specific reason; it was just a small town, isolated and self-contained. Neighboring Zorn was another world altogether, and as for Brabant or someplace like that—well, that was practically at the edge of the world. A traveler from distant parts was an event, even if a minor one. It didn't matter whether they gossiped about him or not, as long as his trail was indistinguishable from all others. Even if it was a burglar's trail.

"Just let it work out," he thought. But there was little hope of success. It all hinged on luck. He had had a lot of it already, landing in the more or less right era the first time. Right era? If this was just the beginning of the eleventh century, then he had to go back, for there wouldn't be a trace for the antigravitator here. How many other tries would it require? Two, three, ten, maybe a hundred, to get into the twelfth century. The uncertainty principle turned the task into a lottery, with the winning ticket hidden among the hundreds of losing ones (luckily, time travel worked only for a span of a few thousand years). But even an accurate landing—within a century—did not guarantee success. If the antigravitator was not in the city in, say, the twelfth century, it could mean that it had landed in some swamp, or that it had been found and sold as a rarity to a traveling merchant. And then the search would become a puzzle undreamed of by any detective—try to guess in what part of medieval Europe the object was!

Berg smiled involuntarily. He had been chosen not because he was a top specialist or a particularly clever person, but because he was, strangely enough, a particularly lucky man. For most people, success and failure come fairly evenly. But there are amazing exceptions. Some attract disasters as a tall tree attracts lightning, and others repel them—a phenomenon known for ages, but never understood. So far his reputation for luck was holding out.

Judging by the clothes of passersby, he was in the late twelfth or early thirteenth century. He had to know more precisely, and he headed toward the cathedral. If there were statues of saints in the square, then it was the thirteenth already. If not . . .

The statues were there, and they hadn't even darkened yet. That meant that some 150 years had passed from the time the antigravitator had fallen. A period that made the search more difficult. But it was amazingly lucky nevertheless.

Berg had a full view of the square. He looked around. Everything was very gloomy. The dark, crowded facades, the horse neighing around the corner, the pedestrians blending into the dusk, and the foreign speech and clothing all depressed him. A silent group of citizens were crossing the square. They were going to pass right in front of him, and he suddenly realized that in his mood he would not be able to stand the most innocent scrutiny. Trying to be inconspicuous, he slipped into the open doors of the church.

It was clean, uplifting, and almost light inside. By the terms of the century, it was blindingly bright, though for one used to electricity, it was a murky cave. But Berg was getting the feel of the Middle Ages, and he could appreciate the contrast between the church's interior and what was outside it. Candles glowed, spreading light. The organ rumbled softly, and in the flickering semidarkness of the domes he could see gold, and the ascetic faces of saints looking down at him. And the longer Berg looked at them, the quieter and stronger he felt. He tried to smile ironically, but the irony was not convincing. The steady movement of the praying people, the flicker of the candles, the floating sounds made him forget the darkness. It was hypnosis induced by rhythm, color, and sound, and nothing more!

No, there was something more to it. Berg could isolate and appreciate each individual component of what was acting on him, but the sum total was more than hypnosis. Here, now, in the deep Middle Ages, all this served as a safety valve. People experienced the illusion of being at one with themselves, with others, with that mystical being that was there in the church, watching over them and preserving them, chiding and blessing, enlightening and repressing, uplifting and reconciling. A completely different, anxiety-ridden emotional state, and an understandable, but repellent, spiritual world.

After a while, Berg went outside. A cold wind went through him, and he wrapped himself in his cloak. As he turned the corner he almost bumped into a man dressed in rags, barely able to stand on his feet—he was either drunk or sick.

"Listen . . ."

Berg did not turn around, even though something inside him prompted him to help the man. But his training, like a reflex action, forced him to consider involvement out of place, perhaps even dangerous.

"Listen, listen," the man muttered in a monotone, maybe talking to the wall.

He was probably a beggar.

Where should he go? It didn't matter. The contents of his bag, the belts, the clothes he was wearing, and the copper ring on his finger resembled the objects of the distant past only externally. Who would be suspicious of an ordinary flint? Or of a piece of mica? The flint, however, was an infrared flashlight, and the mica made the infrared visible to him. The ring was even more important. It could zero in on the location of the antigravitator. It was cold now. Within a 100-meter radius from the antigravitator it would get warmer. Just as in the children's game—warm, warmer, hot.

He had no weapon. None at all. According to the plan, not one of his actions, even in the most unexpected situations, could risk a change in history. Of course, if he performed a miracle in an age when people believed in miracles, no one would be overly surprised. Every thread stops vibrating with time, and only a break was dangerous. And such a break, leading to the most unpredictable consequences, could be a killing in self-defense. He had to be careful in the minor details as well, because theories were only theories, and who had ever put them to the test? Who would dare test them?

The wind was scattering the clouds. An orange stripe of sunset showed for a few seconds, but couldn't illuminate the tiny winding streets, where the houses huddled together like sheep in bad weather.

It was getting cold. Berg tried to stuff his hands in his pockets, and was very surprised not to find any. So, another detail he had missed! Not watching himself, he had made a gesture that no man in the thirteenth century could have made, simply because they didn't have pockets in those days.

Suddenly his finger felt warm. Berg froze, unbelieving. Would it be that simple? He scurried around the narrow streets, panicking each time the ring cooled off. He gradually calmed down and narrowed his circles until it became clear that the antigravitator was behind the walls of one of the houses.

A light burned in the two tiny windows of the second floor, which extended over the street. The inhabitants were still awake. That didn't matter. Nothing mattered now. A quiet joy of satisfaction spread over Berg. It was almost over now. The city had been sweet, with its tile roofs, its pleasant antiquity, all of it. Berg memorized the layout of the house, the entrances, and checked out the door. People went to bed early here, and it wouldn't hurt to spend an hour or so in a tavern, to observe the life. Then he would return, do what had to be done, and good-bye Middle Ages! He came as a shadow, and he would leave as a shadow, and only the dogs would have been any the wiser. The doctor in the twenty-first century would examine his soiled boots and spattered cape and say: "Well, well, well, you certainly look authentic. Did you bring back the plague as well?"

The sooner the better.

He found a tavern nearby. To Berg's surprise, no one paid any attention to him. They were all crowded around a bench and a lop-eared fellow in new leather pants who was sitting on it. He was turning red from the attention. There was a puddle under the bench. Mugs were held aloft, and jokes Berg could not understand flew thick in the air. It was stuffy and smelly, and soot hung in huge flakes from the rafters. The heat of the coals ran across the overheated faces, shining red on sweaty cheeks, falling into laughing mouths.

No one looked up at Berg as he found himself a seat in the corner. The owner, a stoop-shouldered man of forty with a crooked nose, separated himself from the crowd and asked what he wanted.

"Dinner," Berg said curtly.

"Come from far?" the keeper asked, catching his accent.

"From Brabant."

"Well, well."

The tavern keeper walked away, bowing slightly. Berg followed him with his eyes, and immediately forgot him, because the laughter and talk stopped suddenly.

He could see over the backs of the men. A fat man with triple chins slowly made his way to the youth on the bench. He touched his shoulder, and the boy shuddered, as though electrified. The men shifted and mumbled.

The young man stood up, and to Berg's amazement, the bench rose with him. The boy turned slowly, and the bench followed him, until everyone was satisfied that the bench was stuck securely to the pants. Then a wondrous roar went up.

Berg understood. Why hadn't he guessed right away that the boy had just passed into the ranks of brewers? The candidate had to brew beer, pour a mug of it onto a finely sanded bench, and sit on it in new leather pants. The pants would stick if the beer was good. That meant there was one more brewmaster in the town.

There was something childlike and spontaneous in the festivities. Chewing on the unbelievably tough meat (it sure wasn't synthegrub), Berg felt almost envious. He probably wouldn't be able to laugh that uproariously, reward the fellow with cuffs, pour rivers of wine or beer into his mouth, digest hunks of meat, belch, stamp his boots, and completely abandon himself to the mood of the moment. He called the innkeeper, paid up, and left.

The sky had cleared noticeably. The sky over the broken line of rooftops shone milkily in the spot where the moon was. But it was totally dark below. Berg had gone some ten paces when he saw torches ahead of him.

Berg looked around. Lights were coming toward him from behind as well. Weapons glistened in the light. The night guards.

So what?

The flickering light showed hairy faces, panting mouths, and the steel of knives and helmets. Berg squeezed against the wall to let them pass. Several spears pressed into his chest.

"Keep your knife at his throat!" someone commanded exultantly, and an ursine mass of bodies fell on Berg.

"What for?" he screamed in a muffled voice. "I'm from Brabant, I'm—"

Sarcastic laughter came in reply.

"Try another one! You think you can change clothes and elude us, Berg?"

Berg?

They dragged him off, cursing, reeking of garlic and onions.

The room they finally shoved him into was small. The stone nakedness of the walls was covered with two or three tapestries that were barely visible. There was a smoking candelabra to the left of the blazing fireplace, and a desk and armchair to the right. A white-haired old man in bishop's robes sat in the chair, so dried-out and wrinkled that it seemed as though the massive cross he wore were pushing through his chest. The old man slowly turned his head. Berg could hear the crackle of the guards' torches.

"Closer, bring him closer," the bishop said, his voice like rustling paper.

"I'm not who you think I am," Berg said loudly. "This is a mistake. I've never been in your city, I—"

"I know!" The old man's hand lightly struck the arm of the chair.

"I know how brazen you are—brazen and blasphemous. Did you hope I would believe the rumors of your death? You should be on your knees begging for mercy right now. Execution is no pleasure, do you know that?"

The bishop moved forward. His neck stretched out like a plucked goose's. One of the guards snuffled with a cold.

Surprising himself, Berg laughed scornfully. The bishop's mouth fell open. The shadows created by the torches jumped, and everyone froze in stunned silence. It was all crazy, a wax-museum exhibit that he didn't have anything to do with. He went on smiling.

"The seesaw!" The bishop's head shook. "Tomorrow!"

"What about her?" someone asked. "Her too?"

"And her! Before him! In front of his eyes! In front of your eyes, Berg! Still not shaking? She'll burn on a low, low fire, with that pup she conceived in unlawful union. Think about repenting! Think about it!"

The bishop fell back in his chair. He would have looked like a corpse, if not for his burning eyes. Berg shrugged disdainfully.

He was taken and locked in a little room. The bolt clanged, and footsteps disappeared upstairs.

Berg lay immobile for some time. It was an amazing coincidence that he had turned out to be the double of some local Berg, but there was no point in trying to figure the odds or ponder the theory of probability. It might even be the Berg whose grave—no matter! The thirteenth century Berg had done something serious, his enemies had set a trap, and a man from the twenty-first century had fallen into it. What a situation! It looked as if the innkeeper had turned him in. That wasn't important either. What was it they had threatened him with? Oh yes, the seesaw.

Berg shuddered with disgust and anger. The condemned was tied to one end of a seesaw and lowered into a fire and then pulled out, to give him a respite—that was the seesaw. The slow roasting of a human being.

Bastards, stupid sadists! But he'd show them. They'd dance for him, waving their cassocks. They had the wrong fly in their web. He wished he could see their faces in the morning.

The moon peered out from the clouds with greater frequency, casting a long shadow of the window's bars. Berg rattled his chains and smiled triumphantly. Stupid thick chains of poor-quality metal and the naive bars in the wide window—the jailers had no idea of what twenty-first-century man was and what he could do.

"I don't like this hotel," Berg said. "It's damp and cold. But I guess I can stay to round out my education."

He lay down and shut his eyes. His trained body knew what to do. A dark wave engulfed his consciousness. Now all the cells of his brain and body were following a single rhythm, the awesome rhythm of all the powers of an organism in tune.

Berg pulled. The chains burst.

"There, that's better," Berg said.

What used to happen in one man in a million under great stress was now a power that was harnessed by every inhabitant of the twenty-first century, and everyone knew how to call on the hidden reserve of energy that increased the limits of 'normal' physical strength a hundredfold.

Berg waited for the moment of weakness to pass, got up, shook off the remaining chains, and then tore open the window bars.

Now he had to rest for at least a half-hour. If the guards, attracted by the noise, should rush in now, Berg would have been unable to resist, particularly since he had no defense against spears, swords, and other weapons. But nobody was standing guard under the window or outside the door. Why should they? The chains were massive and the bars dependable.

His room was in a tower. The uneven wall promised a simple descent. Berg waited for the moon to disappear and climbed out the window.

He went down slowly, confidently, like a mountain climber. He had never belonged to these clumsy times with their bizarre laws and accidents. The momentary fright, when he was taken by surprise and trapped, had passed, and after the breakout he sensed himself a man of his epoch again—proud, independent, and powerful.

Berg saw there was a window directly below him. He headed around it. His head was even with the top of the bars when pebbles scattered under his feet. Berg froze, clutching the bars, and just then the moon came out again.

In the chalky moonlight Berg could see someone move behind the bars. Trembling fingers grabbed his hand.

"You came! I knew it, I had faith in you, my darling."

Berg stifled a scream of terror. He saw a young woman, practically a child, behind the window bars. She was reaching toward him, sobbing and smiling, and her whisper was so full of joy that it made Berg's heart contract.

So this was the other Berg's bride, the pathetic girl who would be burned in the morning!

"You're the most wonderful, darling, dependable man, my darling Berg. Hurry, save our child!"

"Our child? Of course." Berg felt as though he were falling through space. He had to get rid of her so that history would not be changed.

The girl was kissing his hands.

"Quiet," Berg said.

He pulled on the bars of the window. There were no crossbars and they pulled out easily from their sockets. He pulled her through the opening. She was dressed in a nun's habit. "So that's it," thought Berg. He was as cold as a robot with her. He picked a spot below, jumped down, spread his arms, and helped her down.

"Our baby is beginning a stormy life," she said, barely catching her breath.

"Let's go," Berg said.

They melted into the shadows of the sleeping streets.

Now Berg had time to think, but he couldn't. What was the point? This girl and her baby were supposed to die at the stake and now they wouldn't; their descendants would live in all ages, which hadn't happened before.

He wanted to kill her and himself.

They reached the city walls. A house came up almost flush to the wall, and there was a dark space between them.

"Wait here," Berg commanded.

He expected remonstrations, surprise, fear, but she merely nodded, even though he could feel her shivering.

"I'll try not to be afraid," she said.

"I'll be back soon," Berg muttered.

Not knowing why, he squeezed her hand. She hugged him for a second and immediately let go.

"You must go, I know. You told me back then that everything would be all right, and that I shouldn't be afraid. And I'm not. But when you get back will everything be like before?"

"Yes, yes."

What would be like before? Berg wasn't too sure where he was running and why. But something was leading him with the accuracy of an automatic pilot, and he realized that his ring was warm again. The house rose above him like a cliff. He felt for the lock. His bag had been taken away when they arrested him, but his belt buckle was a fine tool. He managed to unlock the door and put the mica on like a monocle. The warmth of his hand had turned on the "flint" flashlight. Entryway, door, stairs. Berg waved his hand in the air, and the ring indicated the stairs. The stairs didn't look particularly trustworthy. He took off his shoes. He was as calm as if he had spent his life burgling medieval apartments. The stairs led to a hallway. The house smelled of warmth, smoke, and rotting wood. It was deathly still, except for a mouse scratching away somewhere.

Behind the squeaking door was a room that looked like a museum. Shelves with plants, stuffed animals and birds, hourglasses, minerals, bits of wax, skulls, chalices, rolls of parchment—all this and more lay, stood, and hung in the room, was spread on tables and chairs. His flashlight beam slipped over the objects until it settled on the sooty bugle in the corner. Berg almost sneezed from the dust. Under the bugle, amid the crucibles and pliers, he found the antigravitator crystal, melted out of shape. They had obviously tested it with acid. Of course! It was much too heavy, suspiciously heavy for its size. Berg shoved it inside his shirt, went back downstairs, put on his shoes, left, and locked the door behind him. The hardest part of his mission had turned out to be the easiest.

Now he could think calmly. After all, what was that girl to him? Why was he getting involved in something that wasn't any of his business? Compassion? Of course. But there had been many who were burned at the stake, before today and after. Their fate elicited pity, but it was a cold abstract pity. And he hadn't even thought about the girl until he saw her, even though he had known about her. So what was bothering him now?

Logically speaking, she did not exist at all, just as this whole century no longer existed, disappearing with its hopes and its sorrows. But the future did exist, the century that he had come from and that could suffer from his actions.

But on that dark street the future seemed like another cold abstraction. And that trusting girl was real, that girl whom he would have to betray.

Berg shut his eyes and stood for a moment, moaning with anguish and frustration. But whose fault was it that the need to help and defend came up like a reflex in him? Why, the fault of the very society that bred him.

A pathetic rationalization.

But why pathetic? And why just a rationalization?

When the mind tries to guess the trajectory of a future moral act and concentrates too strenuously on contradictory concepts, the concepts themselves become unclear, because every concept is as deep-rooted and murky in its beginnings as the reality of life that gave rise to it. And the mind falters, determination slips away, and everything seems confused and wrong. That's how thinking can sometimes destroy determination.

Berg shook his head. The weight of the antigravitator reminded him of his priorities.

You can't determine the speed of an electron and its position in space at the same time. And you can't travel to a chosen moment in time and a chosen place. But choice is inherent in life, and saying yes to one thing always means saying no to something else. Doesn't that mean that the roots of morality grow from the same soil as the roots of nature?

Berg's mind raced. Why would history have to be the worse for his behavior? Where does it say that? If his deed was honest and good, it should be just the other way around. Otherwise how can one live and act in the present without the certainty that the good done today will benefit tomorrow? How can you live and function without knowing that? How can you build a future without it? And if it's so, then . . .

"I'm back," Berg said.

She rushed to him with a stifled cry. He held her back.

"We don't have much time. Think—is there a house here where you . . . where we could wait?" Where he could leave her to wait for the real Berg—if he was still alive.

"You know there isn't!" That was that—the compromise hadn't worked. "You . . . you seem different, darling. Have I done something wrong? Is it me?"

"No, no."

"Then . . . I didn't understand everything you said about our love being something unique, that there's never been a love like ours, but now . . . you haven't even kissed me!"

He submitted. And kissing her, he realized that he never wanted to stop, that he wanted to kiss her all his life, that she had been close to him from the first, and that everything else was nonsense with which he had tried to shield himself from his love, in which he hadn't believed but which had bowled him over.

And in his joy he saw the answer, so simple and obvious! The chronoscaph would take them both! The girl had to die in the past, and she would die for the past to live in the future.

What about the other Berg? The hell with him, if he couldn't save her!

He laughed.

"What's so funny, dear?"

"Nothing. It was all true: our love is unique, there's never been anything like it. We will be saved, if you can walk all night."

"It won't be the first time."

"But—"

"The little one is no trouble. He doesn't bother me at all. You see, I don't even show yet. I will walk as far as you say, as long as you are near me."

Berg was infected with her confidence. He unwound his woven belt, threw a loop over the wall, covered the girl with his cloak to keep the ropes from burning her, tied the rope around her, and a half-hour later they were free.

Berg breathed deeply in the forest, which no longer seemed hostile or strange to him. The girl, wrapped in his cloak, walked next to him, and he supported her, feeling the warmth of her shoulders and experiencing a dizzying tenderness. The silver-and-black shadows of the leaves seemed to float through him. Or he was floating on a weightless carpet spreading out before him.

In the flickering moonlight he got a good look at her face, but he still couldn't tell if she was beautiful or not. What difference did it make? None. Just like her past, like the tiny world from which he had plucked her. He even knew how she would react to the future. As if it were a fairy tale, a paradise that her lover had brought her to. She would accept his world with the same courage and determination with which she had accepted her fate, but he would have trouble convincing her that they were still alive and not in heaven. He didn't know why everything had to turn out that way, but he was sure that it would.

Exhaustion suddenly overtook him. He felt that the shadows were keeping him from walking, that they were tripping him up. He stumbled once or twice. It frightened him. Of course, he should be tired after everything that had happened that night; he was going on pure adrenalin. But was he going to collapse midway?

He forced himself to avoid the slippery shadows. But his legs seemed to lose their connection with his body. He didn't even feel them anymore. But his arms were being dragged down by the antigravitator. Everything except his legs got heavy: his head, arms, the girl's body when she leaned on him. And this led Berg to think of something that made him shudder.

"How much do you weigh?" he asked.

"Me? I don't understand."

"Sorry, never mind. I was just . . . "

Of course she wouldn't know, wouldn't understand what he meant. It was ridiculous to think that in thirteenth century girls weighed themselves on doctor's scales, and Berg was embarrassed by his question. He knew his exact weight, and he had estimated hers when he had lowered her over the wall, and there was no question that the chronoscaph could handle both of them. "Don't panic," Berg said to himself. "That's all we need!"

"Let's sit down," he said, even though it wasn't time for a rest break yet.

They sat down, and he could tell by the way she slowly lowered herself onto the spread cloak and the way her eyes stared straight ahead that all her strength had been bravado—she was exhausted, much more exhausted than he—and that she would rather die than admit it. Berg almost moaned aloud and suddenly felt a surge of strength, or of the fierceness that replaced strength.

"Let's go," he said, knowing that a long rest would make things worse, and that neither of them could ever make it alone, but together they would, drawing strength from each other.

They went on, silently in accord, and the night was endless for them because they had pushed their strength to its limits. But the dawn finally came. The dawn promised the sun, and Berg cheered up, even thinking that they would remember this night joyfully.

They reached the top of the hill where the oak tree was still dropping its leaves. Berg thought that it was possible for that oak to live on through the centuries, and he wished that it would last until they came back to rest under its aging branches.

The grass was gray from the thick dew. They were close to the place where the chronoscaph was hidden, disguised as a boulder. They reached the edge of the forest, and Berg decided to take a last break. She lowered herself to the ground, and he almost feared that there was no life left in her body after the prison, terror, and flight, that her consciousness was asleep, that she sensed nothing anymore. But she stirred and looked up at him, seeing something in him that made her straighten up and brush her hair out of her eyes. And that stubborn, willed movement revealed her to Berg not the way she was now—exhausted, with black shadows on her face, in a dull nun's habit—but the way she really was; he suddenly saw her dancing in a white dress. He shivered, the vision was so real—the lithe girl in white, flickering like a candle in the wind. A happy girl afraid of nothing, a child of the twenty-first century. "Well, well," he thought, trying to catch his breath, "I guess the difference between our centuries isn't so great after all."

A distant hollow sound tingling in the dawn's stillness woke him from his reverie. He listened and his heart contracted—hoofbeats. She heard them too, and from the way she tensed and the way her face grew even paler, he knew that she understood the meaning of that sound.

He pulled her hand and they ran, but she didn't have the strength to run anymore.

"I can't! Save yourself!"

He picked her up, not at all surprised that he could.

They stopped at the top of a hill. There were ten men on horseback, and they were less than a mile away. A pack of dogs ran on ahead.

There was still time. He ran, feeling nothing except the searing pain in his lungs and seeing nothing except black streaks, and he was totally concentrating on finding the right bush and boulder in the black streaks.

And his pride stirred as he realized that twenty-first-century man could do the impossible without technological help.

He barely recognized the field in which he had hidden the chronoscaph. The hoofbeats were getting closer, but the riders were still out of sight. His lungs were bursting. He no longer felt the girl's body—rather he felt it was his own heavy, cumbersome, unresponsive body.

The "boulder" opened as soon as Berg touched it. The dogs were on the field, barking and baring their fangs.

Berg put the girl on the seat—he had to pry apart her hands around his neck—and got in himself. The door cut off the barking. Berg pushed the start button.

The motor whined and stopped. Without thinking, Berg pulled on the reverse lever. The chronoscaph jumped—and stopped.

There was extra weight in the antigravitator, which Berg had forgotten to include in his calculations!

Everything that happened seemed to be done not by him, but by someone else. Berg threw the antigravitator in the girl's lap. She tried to say something, or to cry out. He set the return autopilot to the twenty-first century, pushed the start button, and rolled out, shutting the door behind him. As he fell, he saw the chronoscaph disappear.

He lay face down in the dirt for a while, wondering what was taking the dogs so long. The blood was pounding in his ears—that must be why he didn't hear their barking.

No, that wasn't it. He slowly opened his eyes. What was this? The noonday sun poured down on him, birds were singing, and it was spring, not autumn.

So that was it! He got up, reeling like a drunkard. His orderly mind slowly went over what had happened. In his haste to start up the chronoscaph, he had put it into reverse. And the machine had worked for an instant, taking them back in time. And that meant . . .

And that meant that there had been no other Berg in the thirteenth century. It had been he. The chronoscaph could not have taken him back too far in time, so now he was in the years just before his original appearance in the thirteenth century.

Berg looked around at the radiant world which was now his world. He had returned the antigravitator, he had saved the girl, without changing the course of history, but he had also ruined his own life. It was ridiculous to hope that someone would be able to send a chronoscaph to the exact place and time where he was now located.

No, he knew his future ahead of time. The rest of his life would be spent in the thirteenth century. It would become his century, he would live in it, meet the girl he would fall in love with (whom he loved already), bring down the wrath of the bishop, and die a few days before he himself would save her. The old loop of time, according to the theories, when "after" precedes "before." No human had ever seen the grave in which he would be buried, but having slipped into his past and his future, Berg knew how it looked in the modest village cemetery.

It seemed he didn't have long to live.

And still, he had been lucky even in his bad luck, because his life would be a worthwhile one. He would enter battle and win. He would have time to love and be loved. Have time to give happiness to someone who had never dreamed of it. Have time to become a father. And perhaps that was a worthy accomplishment for a man of any era.

# *Final Exam*

THE CALENDAR SAID 2013 A.D., but little had changed: before an exam your palms still got disgustingly wet, your mind panicked, your heart thumped, and time tasted like a flabby eraser.

Someone paced nervously in the hall; someone, staring blankly into space, recited the proofs of Everson's formula; someone flipped through a textbook hysterically; a girl in a sky-blue sweater was holding a mirror to her forehead—a vain attempt to cool off her feverish brain.

"Just imagine, nowadays everyone is expected to pass more than a hundred exams in his life!" a young man next to Pavlov was saying, looking about with his slightly bulging eyes. "Yes, over a hundred! Everyone! I counted. There's forty-seven in school—"

Circumstances kept him from finishing. The door swung open smoothly (for some reason all doors to examination rooms open in a sneaky and sneering manner). There was a burst of confusion and then a bottleneck at the entrance. Some were pleased by this. Sometimes in the crush one could sneak past the proctors who were checking to see if anyone had taken pills to stimulate mental activity. This was strictly forbidden, but there were always one or two in every crowd who thought they could fool the machines with some new combination of drugs. A vain attempt! Smiling in embarrassment, two perpetrators were sent back, swallowing antistimulants as they went. They got a double punishment. First of all, they lost fifteen minutes while the drugs neutralized each other, and second, the mind is rather addled by the process. A lot of people even felt sorry for these hapless descendants of the extinct tribe of cribbers.

Pavlov took a seat by the window. And, as usual, he suddenly realized that his mind was a total blank.

He tried to calm himself. After all, this wasn't an unusual exam. It was the ordinary final exam. He had been preparing for it for three whole days. And he loved Galya much too much to disappoint her with failure. And how was he any worse than the others?

He moved the portable computer console closer and decisively pushed the start button.

A narrow list of questions slid out of the slot. At first the letters jumped around so much before his eyes that he couldn't understand a thing, started rushing, reread the list, stared at it dumbly for a second. Then a wave of calm, broad and warm, spread over him.

The first question was not tricky, though it did require time to answer correctly: "Describe the negative aspects of projection."

Pavlov took a piece of paper. The anxiety was gone and he wrote freely and quickly. "When a man faces unwanted and unpalatable information, mechanisms of unconscious repression and blocking-out come into play, with varying degrees of effectiveness. Projection is one of them. This is an unconscious attempt to rid oneself of an unpleasant tendency by attributing it to someone else or to a group of people. For example, some phenomena well known in the past, such as prudishness, are explained in great part by projection. A person with overdeveloped sexual feelings is certain that everyone around him thinks only of sex. He attributes his own anomalous reaction to this sphere of life to other people. That's why their behavior seems so improper, so dirty, to him, and he remains pure and steadfast in his own eyes. This unconscious psychological process, uncontrolled by reason, is directed at maintaining self-respect. If the man used in the example were to realize the truth, he would lose his self-esteem. But such preservation of the ego demands a high price. The person stops being a complete personality, his reasoning functions are dimmed, and happiness is unobtainable. In certain situations such a man can pose a threat to society.

"The methods of control and treatment are . . ."

Pavlov filled up the page and leaned back in his chair. It looked all right to him. Of course, it wouldn't hurt to throw in a few other examples, but it didn't matter too much.

Waiting half a second, he stuffed the page into the slot. The computer graded the paper immediately and the screen lit up: "Satisfactory."

The second question was a snap. The formula for self-respect. Without a second's thought, Pavlov wrote:

$$\text{Self-Respect} = \frac{\text{Success}}{\text{Demands}}$$

And the red light went on! Pavlov stared dully at the signal. Failure . . . failure . . . failure . . .

Ah, hell, he had forgotten to include the coefficient of social influence! Pavlov winked at the machine and added the correction without rushing. Here, shut up!

The hostile red light was replaced by a green one. And everything around him became pleasant, lively, and Pavlov could hear wheezing, papers rustling, nervous foot shuffles. The examination room, it turned out, was filled with sound.

But then Pavlov started concentrating. There were still two questions to go. He didn't even want to think about the last one, it looked so formidable. And the next one wasn't so easy either— "Give the mathematical expression for the inverse of the reason-instinct relationship"—but Pavlov was sure he could handle it.

He took up pen unwillingly and wrote down the first line of Fillipov's equation, and his surroundings grew still once more, as though they were slowly pumping the air out of the examination room.

Slowly but surely, uncertainty overwhelmed him. He was doing something wrong with the integrals. It was something he sensed rather than knew. The connection was unbalanced. It was supposed to be unbalanced. But this much? Pavlov wavered. He couldn't remember how it looked in the textbook.

He wiped his brow and went over what he had written. And the more he checked it, the more mixed up he got. He was beginning to doubt the simplest things. He found the simplest mathematical operation with approximate integrals suspicious, and he spent five minutes to prove an identity that any schoolboy could have breezed through.

And then, angry, he crumpled up the paper, repeated the calculations, and without checking, stuffed them into the machine.

The red light went on.

Only then did Pavlov realize how tired he was. He wouldn't be able to answer the last question. That meant failure. So what. The hell with it.

He looked around. Bent heads, bent backs, indifferent necks. Alone among the lonely.

Galya would comfort him, of course. She'd remind him of makeup exams, of the fact that they were still young and could wait. Of course they could. But the crummy feeling would remain. And she would cry secretly at night, he knew that.

Damn psychology! Previous generations had managed without it, without these special exams, and nothing happened—they lived, worked, brought up kids. Yes, they managed. And down with education in general. Let ignoramuses flourish. That's a comforting thought.

And yet Galya had passed these same exams.

He read over the fourth question: "You are given the matrices of seven various acts. Determine the level of conformity of the personality. Age 17."

The first step was obvious. He had the computer right there. He had to encode the matrices and determine the level of interrelation of the acts. Enter the average coefficient of conformity characteristic for that age. Seventeen. A wonderful time, when the thirst for glorious deeds and protest boils on the fires of impatience. He could use

Krochek's transformations here. Strange, everything was going smoothly so far. All he had to do was divide the resulting figures by the components. One of them would be conformity—the adaptation to an acknowledged or demanded standard. Just try telling a teenager that he's a conformist. Ha! It's safer to tweak a tiger's whiskers. Yet who's most influenced by fads and fashions? Who's the easiest to turn into a raging mob? The teenager.

Pavlov glanced at his watch. And started pushing. It was almost over. He was even happy. When the clock struck twelve, finished or not, nothing more depended on you. Pass or fail, you were free of responsibility, of the need to struggle and strain your brain.

The freedom of defeat.

Pavlov felt someone looking at him. It was the fellow who had been expounding on exams. He was smiling sympathetically. "Stuck, huh?" He was obviously finished, and resting, arms folded, observing the rest.

Pavlov gave him a dirty look and clenched his pen so hard that his knuckles whitened.

The pen took off like a runner in the 100-meter dash. Without looking it over, he stuck the paper in the slot, snorted, seeing the yellow signal, and with a ferocity that amazed him, attacked the damned third question again, feeling the blood thumping in his temples.

He redid his calculations and tossed in the answer so fast it seemed he was trying to rid himself of the shame.

Actually, that's just what he was doing.

The signal didn't have time to light up because it was a fraction of a second after noon. The huge auditorium sighed, moved, and talked. Pavlov was wiped out. He looked at the signboard, where the names of those who had passed lit up. There was an uproar in the room.

Clumsily, trying not to draw attention to himself, Pavlov headed for the door. He was trying to see nothing and hear nothing. Not the exultant shrieks, not the whispers, not the kisses the girls were exchanging as the board lit up with more and more names. It had nothing to do with him anymore. Even if he had handled the third question right, the computer, it seemed, hadn't registered the answer, and the other results didn't give him much hope. A skipped question could only be salvaged by two greens, and he didn't have them.

He walked down the corridor, stood by the window, had a little talk with himself, and returned to the auditorium only when everyone else was gone. He didn't want witnesses to his failure, which, he finally admitted to himself, meant a lot more than mere inconvenience.

The name "Pavlov" hit him in the eyes as soon as he entered. He stared at the board a few more seconds, and the weather outside cleared up, and the birds started singing, and his head was as light as air.

The machine had registered it in time! And the answer had been right! An intoxicated smile spread over his face. He had passed, he had passed after all.

And he went in to the commission with the drunken smile. But the chairman didn't flinch at his face—he'd seen worse than that.

"I'm happy for you, young man," he said, rising to shake Pavlov's hand. "You've passed the required exams, and now you have the right to bear and bring up children!" The chairman's voice rose. "Society allows you to do this, because it finds you sufficiently mature and prepared for the most difficult and most responsible work on this planet. But you have merely demonstrated a preparedness for future responsibilities, and you still have to prove your ability. Too much depends nowadays on making sure that all our children develop into real human beings."

"I understand," Pavlov whispered. "I'll do my best. Thank you."

The unusually bright and festive light still streamed in through the windows.

# *The Man Who Was Present*

THAT EVENING, as usual, the five of us got together at Valery Granatov's. The sneakiest ensconced himself in the host's armchair, the rest settled for regular chairs, and work began.

We often got together to collaborate on writing adventure stories. At first this method, so common in science and so rare in literature, was just a novelty to us, something that could amuse both us and our readers, but gradually things started changing. Our talents, knowledge, and tastes blended together so well that an independent personality emerged which in part resembled us and in part was completely unfamiliar. We noted with astonishment that it was gaining power over us. It did not wish to be limited to writing stories; it wanted bigger and better things and demanded total abnegation on our part. We either had to lose ourselves in the new personality or separate, and we didn't want to do either. It's one thing to lay out your pocket change for a friendly pastime but another to invest all your capital to catch the two birds in the bush. The scales were swinging back and forth, and tonight could decide everything.

So, we were in a lousy mood. I must note in passing that in working out plot lines we had noticed an interesting quality in the thought process. Soon all five minds seemed to get on the same wavelength. We unfolded scenes rapidly and clearly, without spelling things out to one another; we ignited one another's ideas; plans easily passed from hand to hand, enriched in their travels. In such moments we were happy in that special, rare way that comes from collaborative thought.

And then it would all fall apart. We grew deaf. A trifle that should take only seconds to clear up, demanded unbelievable expenditures of energy. We seemed to be extinguishing one another's thoughts. And if the early wavelength brought us to something special, well, the second phase was all the more depressing.

Unfortunately, work that night began in the second phase. Our imaginations flagged, we spoke empty words, and it was as unbearable as a funeral. I stared at the table lamp's harsh light, and thought that there were thousands of simple pleasures—why suffer for something so ephemeral and probably unattainable? I suspect that we were all thinking that.

"What if our hero begins . . . "Valery mustered up a hopeless idea after a very long and discouraging pause.

But he was interrupted by the doorbell.

His slippers scuffing, he went out and soon returned behind a man who had once had red hair, carrying a briefcase. The man gave us a quick onceover and sat down. I hadn't had time to be surprised by his visit, because Valery had spoken from the doorway in a quavering voice:

"Fellows, what if . . . "

And what he said was so marvelous that we forgot everything else and were numbed by joy.

And it worked. All I remember of that night is a general impression of concentrated bliss, as though we were mountain climbing and every step revealed new breathtaking vistas. We were no longer writing a story; we saw a life through and through, we delved into the secret thoughts of people who sprang up mysteriously, we admired and were shocked by sudden shifts in their behavior, captured their every action and word, and we only had to write it all down. It was no longer clear which was more real, the smoke-filled room in which we sat or the world that came alive in our imagination.

And I no longer existed, we no longer existed. There was only that common person who had dissolved all of us within him, who had raised himself above it all and had a special, unparalleled vision. I have never experienced anything like it before or since. It explained life better than any textbook; we understood everything, knew everything, and could do anything, like gods.

Only in the rare moments of relaxation, when the reality of that room penetrated slightly into our consciousness, did I remember the stranger and look at him for a quarter of a second. He was sitting sideways, squinting and rubbing his hands, as though before an open fire. "Fine, fine," he muttered. I didn't have time to examine him thoroughly, but he gave me the feeling elicited by old household objects—a feeling of coziness, dependability, and necessity. I had time to be surprised. Usually, an outsider interferes with concentrated mental work, but his presence was not in the way.

Everything that we did that night was good. We did not ask ourselves if we were developing the plot the right way—we knew that there was no other way. We did not pick words for descriptions—they came on their own, the only right ones, growing from within.

When we finished, it was after four in the morning. We knew that we had done everything, that there was nothing else to do, and that everything that gave the work depth and truth was already on paper.

We looked at each other, with no desire to talk. We were pleasantly drained. The man with the briefcase was no longer in the room; he had disappeared quietly. We put on our coats without thinking of him.

Our host, tossing a coat with a narrow velvet collar over his shoulders, accompanied us. I asked him in the creaky elevator:

"Valery, who's that friend of yours who spent the entire evening with us?"

Valery looked surprised.

"My friend? First time I ever saw him. He said he was looking for one of you."

We looked around. No one had ever seen him before.

"What's going on?" Valery worried. "This is crazy!"

"But you let him in!" we chorused.

Valery's eyes clouded over as he tried to remember.

"Yes . . . I did let him in."

"Without asking anything?"

"He said hello. I wanted to ask him, but then I got the idea for the story, and I just let him in. And then I had no time for him."

"All right," I said, stifling a yawn. "Anyone care to explain?" We were in the vestibule, where doors led to a fish store and a dairy shop, so that it smelled of both milk and fish.

No one could explain it. People just don't drop in on strangers. People just don't spend half the night with strangers. That's as far as we got.

The strangest part was that the mystery didn't worry us too much. We weren't in the mood for it.

"Writing adventures, we ended up in one ourselves," someone joked weakly.

We gabbed about it a little more and then parted, exchanging tired, puzzled smiles.

Many months went by, which in no way solved the mystery, and then I suddenly bumped into our stranger in broad daylight.

Strange, but I recognized him immediately, even though he was wearing an old sheepskin jacket, which made him look even more squat. Before this meeting, I hadn't been sure that I could recognize him even in the double-breasted suit he had worn that night.

"Hello. I had a question for you," I said and strode purposefully toward him, because his eyes had cleared up my last doubts.

He glanced at me meekly from head to toe, and the hand holding the briefcase jerked, as though he wanted to hide behind it.

"Hello," he said in a high-pitched voice. "How's your story going?"

"Marvelously," I said, without exaggeration. "Forgive my nosiness, but who are you?"

"I have a dull name. Fedyashkin. Pyotr Petrovich."

His face matched his name. He had faded, yellowish lashes and brows, flabby old cheeks, and a fat nose.

"You're going to ask more questions," Fedyashkin said sadly, looking away. "Maybe you shouldn't. The important thing is for the story to go well."

He even looked around for a chance to melt into the crowd. There was no way out. I had him up against a wall.

"Excuse me, Pyotr Petrovich, but you do understand why I'm interested. In my place you would ask, too."

"I know. But I can't explain a thing."

"You won't?"

"Honestly, I can't! Did my presence bother you? Why do you need to know anything else?"

We all love mysteries in books and hate them in life. I'm no exception. After all, the reason we love mysteries in books is that the secret is revealed on the last page.

"No," I said firmly, even though I understood the ridiculousness of the situation. "You must explain."

His round body contracted, and there were folds in his sheepskin jacket.

"You won't believe me." He looked around unhappily.

"I'm listening."

"You called me yourself."

"We did?"

"Your thoughts."

I shuddered. His mouth was drawn into a pathetic and yet triumphant smile.

"You see, I warned you. You don't need to know."

Fine! Fedyashkin was a nut.

I took myself in hand and said calmly, "Go on."

No, he didn't want to go on, thinking that I would let him go now. Wrong. For some reason, I was even prepared to shake him by the scruff of his neck to get out the rest of his confession. I even made a mental move toward it. He winced as though he had read my thoughts.

"Don't!" he shouted. "You'll only freeze. All right, I'll tell you, and then you let me go, OK? Young man, you use your brain lightly."

"All right, so you're a telepathist. Go on."

"No! I don't know how to read thoughts. But I sense them, when they're . . . You see, I'm not an educated man. But when someone thinks, then the . . . potentials in his brain change, he emits brainwaves. And when the mind is aflame in creation, it gives off . . . warmth. It's so nice and warm! I mean, I barely notice it, it's just a background. But if it's really burning well, the way it was with you people, then I'm drawn to it."

"That's all interesting," I interrupted. "And very scientific. But you certainly do contradict yourself."

"What do you mean? It's impossible!"

"No, it's not. When you arrived our thoughts were barely glowing, certainly not burning. Right?"

Fedyashkin was embarrassed. I was beginning to like that little psycho. Not only was he harmless, but he was rather touching in his fantasies. But why had he come to see us?

"There's no contradiction," he said uncertainly. "Please don't take this as bragging."

"What do you mean?"

"What do you see around us?"

He waved his arm feebly. I followed his gesture. Tense people went about their work and errands, traffic meandered through the streets, pigeons strutted along cornices and ledges, and a trolley, turning onto the main street, whined and squealed.

"So, around all this there is a cloud of thoughts," Fedyashkin confided, lowering his voice mysteriously. "But there are few hot spots nowadays that mark the creation of something new. That's why each jet of flame is so valuable. And I have the ability—but please don't think I'm bragging now. My presence fans the flame. Didn't you notice that yourself? No, no," he exclaimed, defending himself. "I'm nothing, just a retired accountant, but I have this ability, to help others think. That's why I came to you. I go to many people. That's as it should be. It's better for them, it's good for me, for the world. You don't believe me?"

Of course I didn't. Not a bit. But there was a tiny crack in my solid disbelief: his words could explain what had happened that night.

"Fine," I said. "Prove it."

"What for?" he said bitterly. "You won't believe it anyway."

"I will," I said stubbornly, and illogically I believed that I would believe.

"Let's go," Fedyashkin said.

I was too amazed to argue. We turned down one alley, then another and another. Fedyashkin walked at a moderate speed but with great confidence, and his face looked as though he were listening to distant music.

"Where is it that we're going?" I finally asked.

"Don't bother me!" Fedyashkin barked.

Then he covered himself with contrition from head to toe.

"Forgive me. I don't know myself—somewhere around here. Of course, we could have dropped in at the institute, but you need a pass. But we're almost there!"

I merely waved my hand and tried to figure out how I had gotten involved in this adventure.

Now we were taking back yards and side alleys, and then we went up a stairway, perfectly ordinary and littered with scraps of paper by the incinerator shafts.

Fedyashkin stopped in front of a door on the seventh floor.

"This is it."

He was visibly nervous; his lips were white, and like a turtle he was trying to pull his head into his shoulders.

The bell jingled uncertainly.

A grumpy fellow in a sports coat answered the door.

"Who do you want to see?" he asked indifferently.

I looked at Fedyashkin. He was pathetic.

"We would like . . . " he muttered. "We're from . . . you are working, aren't you?"

"We are," the fellow confirmed.

And then something changed his face. It became completely wrapped up in thought, the way Valery Granatov's had that night when he came back from answering the door.

"All right, you can explain later," he mumbled impatiently, and I could have sworn that he no longer saw or thought about us. It was all very strange.

He didn't even wait for us to take off our coats, but disappeared through the door, beyond which came exclamations, laughter, and then total concentrated silence. And when we went in, we saw three men hunched over a table spread with blueprints. There were blueprints on the floor as well.

The next hour was the most fantastic I have ever spent. Fedyashkin and I sat quietly in the corner, and the men, paying us no mind at all, worked in some sort of controlled frenzy. I smoked nervously, expecting us to be tossed out on our ears at any moment. But they had no time for us, and I think even Napoleon himself could have shown up and gotten no response from them. They tersely exchanged radioelectronic terms, arguing sometimes, but mostly they wrote in silence, and there was nothing in their behavior that suggested external inspiration, rather just deep concentration. Fedyashkin was in quiet rapture, glowing with pleasure; he loved those men and had forgotten about me.

Then he touched my elbow.

"Let's go—they're finishing up."

"What are they doing?" I whispered.

"How would I know?" Fedyashkin whispered back. "Inventing something. Let's go, please!"

I hurried down the stairs in total confusion.

"Everything worked out fine," Fedyashkin said, tripping on the steps. "Oh, they did something magnificent today. How wonderful that they let us in. You know, sometimes people don't let me in. Rarely, I'll admit, I seem to have an effect right away."

I wasn't really listening to his muttering, because I was trying to bring reason and order to my thoughts. I managed to a certain degree. It's absolutely necessary to do that—a defense mechanism. We take any miracle and explain it away through things we understand, in order to spare ourselves the burden of psychic overload. Then, as we get used to it, we become bolder.

My thought process, as I followed Fedyashkin, went something like this.

He's not a nut. His presence, it seems, really does stimulate the creative capabilities. All right. So what? For millions of people, that's what you would call a profession. Teachers do not produce anything of material or intellectual value themselves. They transmit knowledge, and most important, stimulate the mental and moral growth of children—real teachers, of course. That is the great meaning of their profession, to disseminate their thoughts and actions in such a way that they interweave like a golden thread in someone else's life and then come alive unrecognized in the discoveries and achievements of the future—a profession of utmost importance for society. And are teachers the only ones to do this? Like the body's atoms which never die after death, but enter into a new cycle, spiritual movements transmitted by others exist forever, invisibly moving from generation to generation.

But that's not all. Catalysts function in inorganic chemistry—mysterious connections that do not enter the reaction but give it energy and power. Organic processes are catalyzed by enzymes. Why shouldn't there be catalysts and enzymes in psychic phenomena? Why not? I repeated over and over like a parrot, staring dully into Fedyashkin's back.

A new thought sped up my step.

"Listen!" I said, grabbing Fedyashkin's arm. "If you, um, stimulate other people's mental processes, why didn't I feel that right away when I ran into you on the street? Or don't you work on singles?"

He did not free his arm (in general, his actions were marked by great docility). He answered, blushing, but with dignity.

"No, I can help solitary thinkers as well. But were your thoughts anywhere near creativity when we met?"

He looked at me with an apologetic smile.

"Don't, don't demand an explanation. I don't know it myself. I never amounted to much in life. I don't have great talents. I merely accompany great thoughts, and in this way consider myself helpful. I help people think about important things. It's nothing that I have any control over. It's like having a good singing voice—some do, and they sing well. Those that don't will never sing, but they can learn something else. Before, I used to be afraid to go to strange people's houses to warm myself and warm up others. I know my death is near, so I hurry to do what I must, and I've stopped worrying that they'll throw me out like a beggar. And everything is working out just fine. But I don't know why or how. And I find joy in the fact that lately, with each passing year, we have more and more bonfires glowing. I wouldn't be able to get to all of them even if there were ten of me. But what saddens me is that I have no effect on moral fires. I don't have the talent for it. But my late brother did. Ah!"

"Wait!" I was in the throes of a discovery. "If there are people like you who stimulate, then there must also be dampeners?"

"And how," Fedyashkin noted sadly. "Of course there are freezers. Haven't you ever met any? Well, if you'll excuse me, I'll be on my way. I live nearby."

I shook hands with him and watched his rounded body lumbering along on stiff legs. And only when he was gone did I realize my foolishness and curse myself. I hadn't asked him a millionth of what I wanted to know. I hadn't even gotten his address.

But that was no problem. I could look in the directory.

I was in a state of clearheaded inebriation all day. Everything made sense in my hypothesis except for one thing. It was incontrovertible that there were people whose presence speeded up any project—I had known people like that myself. But their influence was always felt in concrete terms. In words, gestures, laughter. They participated in the work, they were not merely present! But Fedyashkin was just there.

The achievements of science have trained us to turn to scientists with the slightest problem. And that's just what I decided to do. I imagined calling Professor X, seeing Academician Z, and both of them rushing to see Fedyashkin. But I sobered up immediately. Professor X and Academician Z could do nothing. People with strange and amazing capabilities were known to science. A man appears who can figure the cubic root of a six-figure number faster than any computer. Or news comes of a man who never sleeps. Who knows how much there is in people that is absolutely unbelievable? But has science tried to figure it out? A human computer can convince anyone: you can see the results of his phenomenal talents right there on the blackboard! You can study him—and people do. And then what?

But Fedyashkin couldn't even demonstrate his abilities. They couldn't be expressed in numbers or other equally concrete and convincing ways. You could either believe or not believe in Fedyashkin, and faith is no proof for science.

Finally I decided that I would look up Fedyashkin, spend an evening or two with him, and see what happened.

But first the galleys of my book came, then I was sick, then there was important business—I don't remember what exactly, but I couldn't put it off. It wasn't that I forgot Fedyashkin, but the whole affair faded somehow.

But I met him nevertheless.

This time, too, I ran into him on the street. It was an unusually hot May, early in the month; the asphalt melted in the sun, though the trees hadn't come into leaf yet. There was something odd in the hot sky that showed through the winter-bare branches. Fedyashkin was slouching, and his wrists hung out from his sleeves. He walked past me without noticing, and I had to call out to him.

He shuddered, looked at me in a lost way, and recognized me distantly, as though I were a speck on the horizon.

"Are you ill?"

"No, why?" he asked uncertainly. "I'm just chilly."

"In this heat?"

"What about the wind?"

I looked around. There was no wind and the city flags hung limply.

"Don't you feel it?" Fedyashkin reproached me. "It's blowing . . . it's been blowing for a long time, but especially hard today. There's a chill over our ancient and wise culture. Don't you—oh, forgive me! I forgot, you don't get the *dernier cri* in thoughts."

"What are you talking about?"

"But why don't you sense it? How dare you not sense it? Reason is being frozen out, it's writhing and dying. And you're warm?"

Fedyashkin roared at me, and then wilted. I said nothing, shifting uneasily from foot to foot.

"The death of a scientist's thought isn't so bad," he continued in a whisper. "It's indestructible, do you understand? If there had been no Newton, gravity would have been discovered anyway, and if there had been no Einstein the theory of relativity would be with us anyway. But what if there had been no Leo Tolstoy? We could search around for centuries, but even eternity would not give us *War and Peace*! Nothing, no one, never will the future make up for such losses! That's the whole trouble!" Fedyashkin's voice grew firmer. "That's why humanity will die in someone, thought will not awaken in someone, someone will not be warmed. But even in science it can be horrible! Just imagine how things would have been held up if Marx's thoughts had been frozen! No, you can't possibly understand how I feel—what it's like to hear the death cries of thought, to hear pleas of help with hopeless despair, unable to do anything!"

"Calm down," I said.

But Fedyashkin couldn't calm down. He cried like an old man, sobbing. People stared at us on the street.

I led him to a soda machine like a child, fought through the line, gave him a drink, and wanted to take him home.

"I have no time!" he screamed passionately when I told him my plan. "I'm going to see those who still think. Don't hold me up! I have to get there in time!"

I barely managed to get him to agree to another meeting.

But it didn't happen. He died that day, as I later learned, collapsing on the run. He was hurrying somewhere. Passersby picked him up, and his neighbors buried him, since Fedyashkin had no relatives or friends. He died as he had lived, quietly, and no one noticed that Fedyashkin was no more. A man with the strange talent of augmenting other people's thoughts. Even I didn't feel a loss, only sadness and a certain disappointment that he had never crossed my doorstep when I had been working, and now he would never cross it.

The story we had written in Fedyashkin's silent presence was very successful, but of course, not one of us acknowledged Fedyashkin publicly. I did thank him in my thoughts, feeling rather uncomfortable as I did.

And that's all. Life is full of situations cut short, unfinished observations, everything that doesn't fit in the parameters of a story that would make sense to strangers. We keep them to ourselves and we carry them away with us.

And that's what I would have done with this story if it hadn't been for yesterday's paper. It carried an interview with a man who had made an outstanding discovery, and it contained the following line: "I give particular thanks to P. P. Fedyashkin, who helped me attack the problem."

There was nothing else about Fedyashkin, but it touched me deeply. Someone had remembered him and was grateful, and I hadn't had the generosity. It was as though I had silently agreed that the ability to help others think was less valuable than other abilities. I had to write about Fedyashkin, whose presence was just as unnoticed and just as necessary for life as the presence of enzymes is necessary for the health of the body.

# Modernized Hell

STEPAN PORFIRYEVICH DEMIN, a man of fifty with a dull gaze and mousy gray in his hair, was an utter bastard. So it was no surprise that one fine day a devil appeared before him.

The clerk from hell wore an excellent wash-and-wear suit, a white nylon shirt, and a silvery tie. There was an elegant attaché case in one paw and an American cigarette glowed between the claws of the other.

"You have committed exactly thirty-three base acts," he announced to Demin, "and therefore we are empowered to take your soul."

"Just a minute!" Demin countered, without even offering his guest a seat. "As far as I know, the limit of base acts—"

"Absolutely correct! But just last month, Hell's directorate cut the limit in half."

"But that's illegal! Arbitrary rule!"

"You're right again. It is illegal. In many parts of the world, illegality is in fashion. Fascist takeovers, constitutional violations, juntas of all kinds . . . . there's no end to it. Hell is trying to keep abreast of things in general and evildoing in particular."

"You could have warned us."

"Don't be absurd! It would no longer be pure arbitrary rule then, would it?"

The devil smiled gently and sat down, flicking his tail. Demin nodded, but suddenly a thought came to him.

"Your papers!"

The devil tossed his ID on the table.

Demin put on his glasses, compared the devil's face with the one on the photograph, picked at the seal of Hell with his fingernail, and returned the document with a sigh.

"Now I would like to hear about the rules governing taking of souls," he said, staring through his glasses.

"Don't worry, they're not complex. First of all—"

"None of that. You must have a rule book."

The devil frowned.

"Damn bureaucracy!" he muttered. "Science has proved—"

"Science is science, but paper is paper," Demin lectured. "Why should I take your word for it? That's not how I do things, and I hope that's not how it's done in Hell."

The devil bowed his head in acquiescence and took out a weighty tome from his attaché case. A fiery word glowed on the spine: "Instructions."

Demin lost himself in studying it. Wheezing with pleasure, he would raise his eyebrows in puzzlement from time to time, mutter, then delve deeper into the text. His usually dull eyes shone, as though irrigated with sparkling water.

The bored devil was losing his patience. Lolling in his armchair, he turned on the TV to watch a hockey game. He was so enthralled by it that he lit two Camels at once and turned up the volume full blast.

"You're disturbing me," Demin noted.

"Marvelous," the devil replied without looking up. "Obstacles are created so that they may be overcome. Don't you agree?"

Demin took a sidelong glance at the devil's twitching tail and said nothing. He was a master of creating obstacles himself. Giving the devil a withering stare, he resumed his reading.

"Yes," he said finally. "A well-written book. And I had thought that the agreement had to be signed in blood."

"Obsolete, and very unsanitary!" the devil snorted. "Here's a form. Just fill it in, and the deed's done."

He didn't even bother looking up from the set—the game was in its final moments, and the outcome was in doubt. The form jumped out of the briefcase under its own power and settled in front of Demin. He picked it up carefully, reached for his inkwell, and filled in the blanks with his illegible official scrawl. As soon as he had dated and signed it, a big round seal flew out of the attaché case and stamped the document with a thud.

There was a hellish smell in the room.

"So do I have to get ready?" Demin inquired.

"Shut up!" the devil howled, busily cheering the winning goal.

He turned off the TV and turned to his victim with a happy face.

"All filled in? Wonderful. Yes, yes, everything's in order. I like dealing with educated sinners," he said and added his signature with the tip of his nail. "I'll just pop down into Hell, register the agreement, and . . . Don't be upset, old man! 'We're all part of the lost generation,' as Hemingway said. You're all going to fry, you know—in the microwave ovens. *C'est la vie!*"

He waved the agreement, shut his briefcase, and disappeared, saying, "Don't worry, all our tortures are based on the latest psychological principles!"

A minute later he reappeared.

"Look, old man," he said casually, "the agreement will have to be redone."

"Why is that?"

"You filled out the form with a fountain pen. You can't. You have to use ballpoint, or better yet, felt-tip pen. I told you that Hell is greatly concerned with progress in general, and administrative progress in particular. So rewrite it."

"I won't," Demin said firmly.

"What do you mean you won't?"

"Just that. Instead of Hemingway and all that other modern stuff you should have been watching the transaction to make sure everything was done properly."

"But . . . but . . ." the devil said uncertainly. "The limit of your baseness has been reached, and therefore—"

"And therefore, young man, the agreement, once signed by an empowered representative, in the case of a later determination of its noncorrespondence with its legal form, said noncorrespondence coming as the result of chicanery on the part of soul-giver, is liable to rewriting only with the agreement of the latter. And if such agreement is not forthcoming, then the soul-giver enters into a new relationship with Hell, regulated by paragraph Beelzebub-117, which states that the given soul-giver moves up from the ranks of 'utter bastards' to 'low-down scum,' who are allowed a doubled quota of base and vile acts. That's what it says in the rule book, and it wouldn't hurt you to become better acquainted with it."

The devil's horns and hooves blanched.

"But it's just a loophole."

"And you will be reprimanded for not watching it. So begone from my eyes immediately. I enjoin thee with the Instruction Book. One—"

"Wait!" the devil howled, stinking of sulfur. "Your baseness wins this time. But for future reference, where, oh where, did you get the ink? You can't get any for love, money, or an immortal soul nowadays."

"Well, young man, I'm something of a conservationist. Better safe than sorry."

# The Ban

As STIGS carefully developed his thought, the dean's face got darker and angrier.

"Left-spiraling photons!" he finally interrupted Stigs. "Yes, yes, I understand: you are planning to search for left-spiraling photons. Why don't you also investigate the principle of perpetual motion while you're at it? Or the coordinates of the Heavenly Gates? Haven't you read Gordon's book?"

"I've read Gordon," Stigs replied, trying to maintain his calm. "The tests were run eighteen years ago, when Borisov's effect was unknown. Theoretically, there is hope."

"Theoretically!" The dean could no longer disguise his irritation. "But the money I disburse must be for practical purposes. Two million!"

"A million. Gordon's tests cost two million. Borisov's effect makes it possible—"

"I've heard that. But you forget just who Gordon is. Or do you suppose that he's never heard of Borisov's effect? Gordon is great not only because he is the father of the unified field theory. Do you know that he has never been wrong in his conclusions and predictions? Do you know, finally, that Gordon's experiments with left-spiraling photons were duplicated with all possible variations? Fois, Sherrington, Brodetsky—the world's greatest experimental physicists. And nothing! They came up with nothing. Left-spiraling light currents are a myth, the philosopher's stone. A mirage."

The dean was almost sixty, and the harsh lines on his face, strangely enough, made him look younger. His suit was very well cut. But all that had no significance. It didn't matter who the man was in that chair and what he wore. The important thing was that he was in charge of finances, he was in charge of a large group of people, an administrator, and as such he could not condone reckless projects that cost money. Even a doubtful project could not count on his benign attention. But Stigs did not lose hope. He would have preferred not to deal with the dean, but even the great Gordon had had to ingratiate himself with people like him in his day. Interesting thought—would Gordon have become the great Gordon if he hadn't done this type of work well?

"It all seems clear to me, Stigs," the dean concluded harshly and moved his folder, signaling that he considered the audience over.

"But you haven't looked at Van Merl's reaction!" Stigs shouted.

"Van Merl? By tomorrow I can have the opinion of ten major professors, and each one will say what I've just told you! You can leave now, Stigs, and get on with your business."

Stigs rose, feeling his hands shake.

"Just one more word."

The dean looked up.

"All right, but no high-flown phrases about the gravity of the problem, the necessity for risk, and like that."

"No, not at all. What if . . . what if Gordon himself says the tests should be run?"

"Gordon?"

The dean leaned back against his chair and tapped his fingernails against one another. He looked at Stigs carefully.

"You're going to try to change Gordon's mind? Hmmm . . . Will he even see you?"

"He will." Stigs knew he was stepping out on thin ice.

"Well, if Gordon agrees . . . then we'll see."

"What luck that Gordon is still alive!" Stigs thought as he approached the great physicist's cottage. "If he were dead I'd have to argue with his authority instead of him, and authority never takes its words back."

Stigs was giving himself a pep talk. The day before, after his talk with the dean, he had begun dialing ten times and hung up ten times before he finally let the call go through. Contrary to his expectations, Gordon had agreed to see him at once. At once! He was a real scientist. Sick, old, cut off—and yet he responded immediately to a call for help! Gordon had listened to Stigs in silence and then a brief second later—Stigs had almost died in the interim—answered briefly: "I'll expect you tomorrow at nine."

Tomorrow! At nine! The living legend was expecting Stigs, treating him, the most average of the average, like an equal. Stigs barely slept all night, rehearsing, rethinking every word, every intonation, going from despair to the certainty that everything would be all right.

And now, at Gordon's door, hand extended to ring the bell, he suddenly felt that his head was empty. He had forgotten everything he wanted to say, he wouldn't be able to put two words together, he wouldn't even be able to move from this spot!

Ugh! Stigs put down his hand. Easy, take it easy. Who was Gordon, after all? A genius on a par with Einstein, but not the Pope, not God, just a scientist, a human being. He had kidney trouble, he liked to breed roses, he was terribly honest, and, they said, kind.

Stigs didn't even notice that he was pushing the bell with all his strength. He didn't remember the door opening and being brought into the house, and taking off his raincoat, and stepping across the threshold.

"Good day. Sit down."

Gordon was half-lying on the couch, and it still felt as though he were towering above Stigs. His head, as majestic as a cathedral's dome, his shoulders towered above him, and the mane of white hair—it was just a cloud floating in an inaccessible heaven. And his gaze seemed to be distant, coming from the icy peaks of great thoughts, a gaze that saw nature's secrets and the misty expanses of immortality. He already was immortal, part of history's bronzes, with a clear, detached gaze.

Gordon stirred and adjusted the blanket on his knees.

"Tell me."

Stigs began speaking without hearing his own voice.

About three minutes later, Gordon stopped him with a feeble gesture of the hand.

"I understand. Wasn't that your article two years ago in *Annals of Physics*?"

"It was." Stigs throat went dry.

"That was an elegant solution of the problem of fluctuation in gravitons. Why didn't you continue working in that area?"

"Because . . . because I saw a bridge there into left-spiraling photons."

"And that attracted you? You can't think of anything else?"

"No . . . I mean . . . not the photons themselves, but the implications."

"And what implications?"

Stigs stared at Gordon. Was he testing him? Mocking him? Playing cat and mouse?

"Movement against the flow of time," he managed to say.

"What else?"

Stigs was completely confused. What else? What else did the great genius see? What secrets were open to his mind, what properties of nature did he mean when he said "else"? What?

Gordon sighed imperceptibly.

"All right. In your opinion, what is the aim of science?"

No, Gordon wasn't mocking him. He was hardly inclined to mockery, Stigs realized. Gordon was looking at him, he was demanding and questioning, gently, persistently, severely.

"The aim of science is knowledge . . . finding the truth."

"What truth?"

"What? Universal truth! Nature—"

"Let's leave nature out of this. Tell me about yourself. Everything, from the beginning."

Gordon closed his eyes.

Stigs, understanding nothing, began apologizing. What could he tell about himself? How he began in science, what science meant to him? You can't explain that. His father drank, there were endless family arguments. That's when Stigs found refuge in books. Primarily in books on science. They took him into the world of pure knowledge, where his anxious spirit soared above the clear fields of truth, where every step brought man to greater heights of knowledge of the universe high among the stars. The gods Newton and Lobachevsky, Darwin and Einstein, Snegov and . . . and Gordon led the boy by the hand. The boy who shut his ears not to hear his mother's cries, his father's drunken curses, the boy who felt dirty from head to toe. How he had studied! What trepidation as he began his first independent research! "The Spin Moment in Degenerate Gravitons." He thought of his gravitons the way one thinks of girls. He wanted to know everything about them, at any cost. There were days when he walked down streets without seeing anything, and when jostling crowds made no impression on him—nothing could impinge on his reality. Somewhere in another dimension there were football games, movies, conversation, money, vulgarity, envy—all the things that had surrounded him as a child—but now, even if he wasn't very good at it yet, he was working way above it all, just as he had once dreamed of doing. But could mere words describe his feelings?

And he couldn't tell if Gordon was listening to him or thinking his own thoughts, or just napping.

Stigs stopped talking. Gordon opened his eyes.

"I must disillusion you, my friend. Left-spiraling photons—a mere illusion."

He sounded just like the dean! Stigs whitened.

"Not everything that is theoretically possible appears in nature. A tantalizing light, a swamp ghost—that's what your left-spiraling photon is. Unfortunately, such lights always glow on the peripheries of science. I chased after one myself, and lost five years—and what years! And so did Fois, Sherrington, and Brodetsky. Isn't that enough victims? You're young, and judging by your articles, talented. Don't waste your time. That's my advice."

"But Borisov's effect . . . You knocked at the front door, and there was nothing but a brick wall there. Maybe the back door is the answer."

"You can't get in through either the back or front door into something that does not exist. As soon as Borisov had discovered his effect I reexamined my conclusions. There was no mistake. Your path is unrealistic."

"But why? Why? Where did I go wrong? How? Show me!"

That was practically blasphemy, asking Gordon for an explanation, frail octogenarian Gordon. Demanding an explanation after Gordon had made it very clear that his word was the truth. But no, in this room that was the birthplace of the unified field theory, this was not sacrilege. Both men were subject to the same law, which was greater than both of them, and that law made it necessary for Gordon to offer substantiating proof. He could not violate it, or else science would turn into religion, and he into its high priest.

"Well then."

There was a pile of paper on the table before him. Gordon picked up a fresh sheet and smoothed it out, and his stiff knotted fingers took up a pen, and mathematical symbols poured out from the pen in strict ranks.

This was the sentence. The ban was shaping up inexorably, and the fence of symbols was stronger than pillars and higher than concrete walls. Gordon was calmly blocking the way for his dream, and the crack of light was narrowing. Feeling a chill, Stigs watched the moving hand write, the confident scratch of the pen, the cruel logic of the proofs. The pen was about to scratch the paper for one last line.

The pen tripped, shuddered, slowed down.

"The rest, I think, is obvious," Gordon said in a tired voice, pushing the paper away from him.

He rubbed his hands and hid them under the blanket.

Stigs thought he was losing his mind! The sentence was written down, signed and sealed, but there was a discrepancy in the proof! A tiny, almost unnoticeable discrepancy. With lightning speed that amazed him, Stigs understood, grasped the chain of conclusions, Gordon's thought processes became his own, he thought it through, and . . .

Impossible! He simply couldn't believe it! The discrepancy could not be explained away. It could not be covered up.

Stigs looked up and almost screamed. It was a different Gordon before him. Bent, pathetic, with a caved-in mouth, and brown age spots on his cheeks. He no longer towered over him, and his dull hair no longer resembled a cloud—Stigs saw him as he really was and not as his imagination had colored him. And Stigs almost cried.

"So you've guessed," Gordon whispered. The old man's head drooped even lower. "You had the daring not to believe me, and now . . . yes, your path is realistic. Realistic, because left-spiraling photons do exist. I discovered that eighteen years ago."

Stigs was speechless. His world collapsed. Stars fell, the sky fell, the gods died. He was dying himself.

Gordon's hand slid out like a lizard from the blanket and touched his shoulder.

"Cheer up. Remember I asked you what is beyond the properties of left-spiraling photons? You didn't answer. You hadn't thought about it. I'll answer. What is the aim of science?"

"What?"

"Man's happiness. If science doesn't make men happier, what good is it? Knowledge is power, a weapon, and if the scientist doesn't care where it's aimed, what makes him different from a mercenary soldier? You didn't think about that, either, Stigs. You wanted to find left-spiraling photons—particles that move toward us from the future. You'll discover them, as I did in my day. And then? Then, practical application. People will learn to see into the future. And to control it, because the natural order of things, once you know it, can be corrected. Will this make mankind happier? Look around you, Stigs. A banker will do anything to keep his capital, or a dictator his power, or a scholar his professorship. Millions of people have a vested interest in maintaining the present order. The future threatens them, because they do not know what will come. They try even now to affect it, in vain. You are giving these people power over the future. They'll destroy it, Stigs."

"But—"

"Quiet. You haven't understood. They will destroy it, Stigs. Roger Bacon, having discovered gunpowder, hid his invention from everyone, for he foresaw what it would lead to. A noble but futile gesture. Fifty years ago, physicists imposed self-censorship to keep their work on splitting the atom from getting into the hands of the Nazis. But they turned over their information to America. It ended with Hiroshima. But even if they locked up their laboratories, there would have been others who would have discovered the bomb. It doesn't have to come from a sense of patriotism. All you need is pure curiosity. Thinking over the lessons of the past, I decided on a different course of action when I discovered left-spiraling photons. I declared that they did not exist. I told world science that it was pointless to look for them. My proof was in my experimental results—falsified. And my authority. I laid it down like a barrier across a path. Oh, I didn't fool myself, I knew that sooner or later there would be a young man who wouldn't be impressed by my ban. But I had to win time. Luckily, experiments to discover left-spiraling photons are very expensive. I had to keep it off for as long as possible! Just fifty more years—even less!—and the world will change. People will look into the future only to be forewarned about natural disasters and to cure diseases before they appear. I believe that. I violated the laws of science. But not those of goodness! And it is not up to you to judge me!"

"I'm not judging you," Stigs said with difficulty, as though he needed air. "But what about Fois, Sherrington, and Brodetsky?" he shouted.

Gordon tossed his head.

"The late Fois, the late Sherrington, and the late Brodetsky were friends of mine," he announced majestically.

And suddenly Stigs felt small again—small before this old man whose gaze was full of proud dignity, whose face was just the way Stigs had seen it on the pages of his school textbooks.

# *What Never Was*

THE YELLOW, HAGGARD, no longer human face was drowned in the pillows. The body under the blanket was so thin that it seemed that the head existed independently. Not even a head, a severed part of a mummy, a wax mockup, a moulage with carelessly attached thinning hair.

"Setti Tovius, attempted suicide, ten tablets of pectalan, all usual methods taken, situation hopeless," the doctor on duty mumbled.

The professor silently examined what had been Setti Tovius just yesterday—a human being, who worked and paid taxes—and who was now a semi-corpse. It followed all the laws. The environment culls the weaker forms: it was thus billions of years ago with the amoebas and algae, and the same thing continued today. The environment of nature, the environment of society, it didn't matter—the culling went on anyway.

"Absolutely hopeless?"

The doctor nodded.

"Well," the professor said, "let's try arguing with nature."

The doctor didn't understand, but smiled just in case.

"Something new?"

"I guess so. Joy and happiness, as you well know, are more effective than any medicine. The problem is, how do you make someone relive moments of happiness when he prefers the company of the dead and is almost dead himself? Is the family here?"

"He has none."

"Friends?"

"Not a single call yet."

The professor sighed.

"There, you see, is the paradox. A man lives in the middle of a big city, goes to work, and who is he really? Robinson Crusoe, a social Crusoe, who's given up hope of ever sighting a sail on the horizon. All right, to hell with sentiment. We have to try the biowave method of creating happiness."

"Artificial dreaming?"

"Formally, yes. But he will experience it as reality. And if after that he doesn't try to recover . . . well, then . . . but no, I believe in successes."

The professor gave orders over the phone, took out a pack of cigarettes, counted them, shook his head ruefully (it was still morning, and half the pack was gone), and lit up. "There's another paradox," he thought to himself. "I work on minimizing the harmful effects of the environment, and what do I do myself? I'm committing slow suicide, pumping my lungs full of smoke."

Setti Tovius moved the springy branches of the pine trees aside. The sea air hit his face, and the white, clean, sparkling, endless shoreline entered his consciousness like a bolt of lightning.

He did not believe it. He squinted and turned to Renata. She was looking at it with wide-open eyes, and her thick hair fluttered like wings in the wind.

Their hands met.

It was about twenty feet to the sea. They walked, hand in hand, and they were surrounded by the pale-blue sky, the shimmering sea, the deserted beach. The gull's cries drowned in the vast uninhabited space.

Something ancient and forgotten stirred in Setti. It was like a crust falling off, and each cell of his body began feeling the warm breath of the sea.

The flat waves licked the smooth compacted sand. Their transparent flow left a melting lacework of foam, but there was something else, something he couldn't identify, in the inexorable steadiness of their action that made it hard to take his eyes off them.

Ten minutes must have passed, maybe much more, and they still stood quietly. Then Setti tossed off the backpack from his shoulders and sensed a wonderful freedom in his body. On the left the beach ended in a promontory; on the right it went off into the blue distance, and there wasn't a single footstep on the entire expanse. It was as though they had fallen out of time, out of the circle of daily responsibilities.

He even shuddered at the thought that the whole shore and the whole sea belonged to them alone and that they belonged only to each other.

"I'll get the bathing suits."

He bent over the pack.

"What for?" Renata asked.

He laughed. What for indeed? She had realized before he had that it was their beach.

He watched Renata undress, baring her shoulders, back, breasts, and he felt nothing other than overwhelming tenderness. The graceful lines of her body were a miracle, and the naturalness of the movements with which she exposed herself, her arms tanned from the sun, the smooth curve of her hips, shaking off the last of her clothes to the ground, and her little smile—it was all marvelous.

He also undressed, and the touch of his bare toes on the silky sand excited him, as a childhood memory.

He did the crawl for a few stormy yards—otherwise he would have exploded from the joy of living that was brimming within him—and then he could calm down, watch the ripples travel over the sandy bottom. Or roll over and float on his back in a briny bed, seeing nothing but the sky and sun.

But even then he sensed the nearness of the girl. And there was an enchanted circle that kept him from getting close to her. Something could crack and change in this world with just one wrong word or clumsy move. Or turn out to be the greatest bliss, if everything went naturally.

A bird as white as sea salt whizzed by him on taut wings.

And he laughed for no reason. And thought of how he and Renata lived there, cooking dinner over a fire, lying down under cover of night, how the pines rustled outside their tent, how the sun rose over the smooth blue sea, and how it all lasted a long, long time—just as long as they wanted.

Renata was standing in the water some distance from him, reflections running across her face. He dove, and when he was almost out of breath, his spread fingers finally found the smooth, firm flesh, and he rose up, knocking over the strong thrashing body of the girl. Splashes, sunshine, a scream, her laughing lips so close—and another dive into the deep and then all of it once again—the blinding splash of water in the eyes, the girl's laughter, struggle and laughter, and a rainbow in the sun.

He grabbed Renata, held her struggling arms, and suddenly her resistance stopped, and all of her—long and lean and warm, suddenly soft and small and trusting—pressed close to him, head back, lips parted. And everything floated before his eyes, and nothing was left except the cool sea, their embrace, her face, happy, mysterious, near, dear and waiting.

And then they parted.

Everything was back in place—the beach at midday, the scent of the pines and the sea, the drops of water in Renata's hair.

They left the water, let the hot sun dry them, and without saying a word, walked along the edge of the tide.

They no longer needed words. Not only their actions, but their thoughts were as one, and their happiness was unlimited. He walked next to Renata, watching her darling footprints in the sand,

and he suddenly dropped down to kiss them. Renata stopped, ran her fingers through his hair, and pulled. He looked up at her, an eighteen-year-old wise child, and his heart beat fast. He stood up, caressed her cheek with his hand, and walked on.

He had known before that she was beautiful, but it didn't matter now. He had loved her agile, fresh body before, the mobility of her lively face, her open, trusting smile, and the tender depths of her brown eyes, but that wasn't it either. If it were just that, he could feel that way about many women; but now she was the only one, and they belonged to each other forever.

The white quartz sand was clean and fine. A myriad of tiny shells crunched under their feet. There was a water line of objects tossed out by the sea: dark smooth pieces of wood, lacy patterns of seaweed, milky burnished glass, opaque fish scales.

They turned toward the pines, into the dark, sandy desert that breathed hot onto their feet. With an anticipation of discovery they neared the forest and found a stream that poured into the sea. It was transparent, warm, and full of tiny fish. They walked in the water and wandered upstream, until the stream widened and the water grew cooler, revealing that its source was nearby, hidden in the greenery. They pushed aside some branches and found it—a bright spurt of water set in damp mosses and dark, glistening rocks.

Without planning it, they lay on their stomachs on the moss and blew bubbles in the water. The reflections of branches and the sky trembled on the surface. Their teeth began to ache from the icy water, and they shivered, and they bounded up to the sunlit meadow beyond the forest.

It was obvious that their home, their tent, would be there. They were surrounded by warmth and the pine smell. They could see the sea sparkling through the heavy pine branches. Setti glanced at the girl and saw that she was standing, eyes shut, her face almost asleep. He closed his eyes, and their shoulders touched. They jumped, as though hit by electricity, and their hands met. And then, as before in the sea, everything swam and floated, disappeared, became dark purple, and there was only the taste of lips, two tongues probing, the giving softness of the earth, and the long, sweet, burning death in each other's arms.

And when it was over, the world was as good as before.

Clouds floated lazily in the sky, Renata's head lay peacefully on his shoulder, pine needles pricked his back. A tiny noise falling from the sky awoke his thoughts. High in the blue a minute airplane rolled and darted.

Setti recognized it even from that distance, and his pride stirred. He was here on earth, but he was up there too, and that was his thought up there, embodied in the streamlined steel body, flying over the planet, conquering wind and distance.

"My baby . . ." he muttered.

The girl understood and frowned.

"How sad that you can't belong to me alone."

But there was no sorrow in her voice. She gave him freedom, asking for nothing in return, admitting, with slight sadness, his right to be himself.

He hugged her gratefully.

"I need you just the way you are. And please don't change."

"I have no intention of changing. I want four children by you. So that I can wipe their noses and buy them toys."

"And a house," he said. "And a yard. And we'll have friends over every evening. No, not every night, I'd miss you too much."

"That's how it will be," she said. "And every morning you'll leave for your engineering office."

"And you'll paint your paintings every morning and be angry when they don't work out."

"I won't get angry. Only talented people get angry."

"You do marvelous drawings. They show the way things really are."

"If that's so, then you'll have an angry wife."

"I'll have a wonderful wife. The best."

"Always?"

"Always."

A ray of sunlight moved over their faces. If you don't shut your eyes tight, the world through your lashes is full of rainbows and mists. The windblown pines sway in the sky and the wind howls in them like a ship's sails. The masts cut through the clouds, and the planet bears you gently on its broad, friendly back. He isn't yet forty, and there will be many days like this one.

Setti Tovius was sitting with his hands in his lap, answering the professor's questions with monosyllables.

"How do you feel?"

"Fine, thanks."

"You know that you've been brought back from the dead?"

"Yes, thanks."

"Well, what's it like?" The professor thought a joke might not hurt.

The patient's head jerked, and the veins stood out on his skinny neck.

"Am I cured, professor?" he asked without looking up.

"Oh, yes! Naturally, this shock didn't leave your organism unharmed. Take it easy for a while! No excitement, no drinking, more fresh air. And no sleeping pills. None! After poisoning like this, even two pills of pectalan could be fatal for you. I do hope you're not planning to repeat this attempt?"

This time Setti Tovius' face contorted into a smile, and the professor felt uncomfortable: it looked as though there were nothing under the parchment skin except bones.

"I was a fool, professor. I was a fool."

"Perfect!" The professor was happy. Now he wanted to finish this conversation as soon as possible. "Well, I wish you all the best . . . in your new life."

He rose. So did Setti Tovius, still staring at his feet.

"Listen, professor . . ."

"Yes?"

"You couldn't . . . that tape with the biowaves . . . the tape . . . could you give me the tape of that life?"

The professor shook his head.

"That's impossible."

"But why?"

"First of all, you need special equipment to run it, which costs hundreds of thousands. Secondly, using it requires strict medical supervision. And third—please understand, this is the most important reason—you cannot live an artificial life."

"Why not?"

"Because . . . but it's perfectly clear! Anyway, the first two reasons are good enough."

"I understand."

He bowed clumsily and started for the door. Damn it, even his suit was worn, and gray, and depressed, like the man himself.

The professor went over to the window. There was the man he had saved walking down the hospital garden. Yes, he had saved him from death by giving him artificial happiness and awakening his will to live. The method justified itself; it would save many others, and bring the inventor fame and glory. Everything was wonderful on that sunny day. The professor was surprised to find a lit cigarette in his hand. He looked into the pack. Sure enough, it was half empty.

The professor was late, and when he got upstairs, he was greeted by the doctor on duty, who told him in his habitual singsong:

"Setti Tovius, second attempt at suicide, all usual methods taken, condition critical, but immediate danger has passed."

"Is he conscious? Can he speak?"

So fast that his coat flew up behing him like an archangel's wings, the professor rushed to the ward where the nightlight barely illuminated Setti Tovius' waxen features.

"Why . . . why did you do this?"

"I . . . wanted . . . the seashore . . . again."

The hoarse voice seemed to be coming from torn lungs.

"My God! But why!"

"Nothing . . . like that had ever happened . . . to me . . . in real life."

"And never will," the professor thought, staring dully at the pathetic object that once had been Setti Tovius.

# *Strangers' Eyes*

THE SUN was no brighter than cast iron, and the planet itself was even duller. Compared to the flat disc of the planet that we could see, the blackness of space seemed to be concentrated light. Looking at the planet, Captain Zibella slowly lowered his thumb. The Romans' gesture for condemning gladiators to death seemed appropriate.

Nevertheless, we were eager to see what the locators would reveal. Irina poured coffee for all of us, but I didn't touch mine. After all, it was the first planet of a black star that we had encountered.

We could hear the telemetrists over the intercom.

"Distance?"

"Distance 0.7."

"Communications activity."

"Zero activity."

The regulations were obeyed unswervingly: the communications activity of the scouting party must correspond to the communications level of the planet. In simple terms, this meant we had to make sure that the planet didn't even have the simplest, most primitive transmitters and receivers that could intercept our signals and therefore discover us before we wished to be discovered.

But the planet, as was to be expected, was quiet.

"Captain Zibella! Permission to turn on the locators?"

"I cannot understand you. Repeat correctly."

Someone sighed deeply over the intercom. Zibella was being true to form. There wasn't another captain as punctilious as Zibella in the entire cosmos. It was a standing joke that his reason for not marrying was that there were no instructions governing the procedure. Maybe Zibella did go overboard, but both people and machines operated smoothly under his command.

"Sorry!" came the voice over the intercom. "Distance, 0.5 in orbit. Communications activity of the objective, zero. Passive visibility of the objective, zero. Asking for permission to use locators, sir."

"I understand you. Orbital distance 0.5, zero activity, zero passive visibility, permission for locator use granted."

All of us, including Zibella, stared impatiently at the screen. The seconds passed, while the computers, testing the space around them, decided on the best radiation for the breakdown and the optimal frequency (frequencies that were harmful to organic matter were forbidden). Out of the corner of my eye, I watched the illuminator; it was still pitch-black. Used to equating vision with light, we found it hard to believe that the locators would function properly.

We were expecting the worst (some atmospheres are impenetrable), and when the picture finally appeared, Irina broke out in a jig. Even Zibella smiled. And why not! It was as if somebody had abruptly pulled back a curtain to reveal high noon.

Leo ran into the control room, rubbing his hands.

"Well, how is it?" he asked, as though he had produced the amazing image without any computers at all.

There was no answer, because just then we saw the huts.

There is little that affects you as much as the sight of a planet you've discovered. Your body and mind become appendages of your eyes, which devour the unfolding view. The jagged chaotic mountain peaks with their unearthly sapphire ice caps. The dots and dashes, looking like bird tracks, that are ravines. The metallic shine of the sea. No one has ever seen it all before. You are the first.

And if you find life, you'd give your immortal soul to get down there faster. But the days of Columbus are long gone, alas. The rule book for uninhabited planets is large enough to kill a man, but it is nothing compared to the one for planets that have life, and perhaps intelligent life. And you can be sure that Zibella followed it to the letter.

We observed the planet from high orbit, medium orbit, and low orbit; did topographical, gravitational, magnetometric, radiolocation, thermodynamic, and other photography, and so on and so forth. We did everything that had to be done, everything that should have been done, and everything that didn't have to be done but wouldn't hurt to do. We almost drowned in the data input.

"Syrup can't spoil pancakes," Zibella kept repeating, who, incidentally, had lost his appetite from the work pressure. But we didn't argue, because the planet turned out to be extremely curious.

Receiving no heat or light from the star, it should have been a dead icicle. But while the climate, according to our standards, was severe, the planet could have been described as flourishing. It got its heat from its own bowels, and the atmosphere retained that heat very well. The vegetation depended on thermal energy, that was clear. But as for the inhabitants of the huts . . .

Orbiting, we couldn't quite make them out. It was only when we moved into the next phase of research, using atmospheric robots, that we got the necessary closeups.

Leo laughed nervously when they appeared on the screen. In body shape and height, the creatures looked like penguins, and their free extremities definitely resembled hands. But as for the rest—imagine a head in the shape of a melon crowned with a wreath. Imagine a pulsating, triangular valve in the middle of the "face." Slits for ears. And no hint of eyes! That's what really kept them from resembling humans—the absence of eyes.

Yet the cone-shaped houses were surrounded with small plots of land with something growing in them. And, on top of that, the houses had doors. Real doors on leather hinges.

Separated from them by many dozens of kilometers, we looked at those doors anxiously, fully realizing what they meant.

"Orchestra, a fanfare, please!" Irina joked, not entirely successfully.

Zibella had paid no attention. He was hunched over a screen across which a small, unimpressive, intelligent creature scurried, and the captain looked as though he wanted to hug the little alien to his broad chest.

But as soon as our first exultant shouts died down, we began noticing inexplicable facts.

The animal bolted when we were only three paces away from it, and ran off on its thin, reedlike legs. But Irina was in its path. She stuck her leg out to block the barrel-shaped body. The animal's horns clinked on metal. It squealed and headed off to the right.

With few exceptions, the animals let us get close to them and then tried to escape by running, not even noticing the most obvious obstacles. We concluded that they heard our footsteps but couldn't see us. Like everything else. Eyeless life. Life in caves.

And they did have real caves here—murky caves. Looking down on it, we had gotten used to the idea that there was a sun shining above the planet, our own radar sun. Now the darkness was depressing us. Darkness and the thoughts associated with it. Vegetation here did not stretch upward, as it does on earth, but huddled close to the ground. The colorless, frail, flat leaves spread out in layers, and the higher up they were, the thinner and wider the dead, funguslike leaves were. A repulsive greenish-yellow slime dripped down from them, as though all the vegetation on the planet had a head cold. It was disgusting to look underfoot, but there was no pleasure in looking at the sky, either. Pallid rags flapped far up in the darkness: the local birds, so to speak. No, this was definitely no place for man.

Following behind the others, I thanked fate that I was only a visitor here. Discovery and research—that was our job. Someone else would have to live here. Because the planet would require an observation station. Years of loneliness and gloom, long, dull years that it would be better not even to think about, even if they were going to be someone else's problem. As I made my way through the slimy plants, I was glad that I had a round-trip ticket.

We approached the huts without camouflage, since there were no eyes to see us and our lights. We could be given away by noise, but we did not plan to get that close.

And yet, from habit, we crept into the "bushes"—some local plant with leaves as full of holes as Swiss cheese. It was funny, if you thought about it, but we were in no mood for laughter. We'd been trying to figure out how this blind world managed to exist.

There was no question that it was blind. Neither the animals nor the inhabitants of the huts had distance vision. They had no eyes, and that was understandable. But they had no organs that could replace the function of the eyes—organs that would allow them to be aware of distant objects, the way bats can, for instance. Hearing? It was no better developed than ours. Smell? On the level of a dog. Some sixth, seventh, or tenth sense unknown to us? We had observed several times that an escaping animal would bump full force into obstacles, just as the barrel-shaped creature had run into Irina's leg.

Of course, it made sense. What was vision for on a planet that was nothing more than a huge cosmic cave?

A wonderful explanation, but it was no good. Because the animals here could run, and run fast. And where there is running, there is vision—otherwise running is sheer suicide.

Everything that we observed here was just absurd, as though a crowd of blind people had decided to stroll on a superhighway. A world like this simply could not exist, and yet it was functioning and flourishing. Well, we weren't too sure about the flourishing part.

Our lights, which were effective at hundreds of meters, flooded a group of huts with bright light. They seemed deserted. We had the impression that it was all unrealistic scenery that had been abandoned by the actors. I kept waiting for the director's voice to tell us the shot was over and we could all go home.

But time passed, and nothing changed. We shuddered when a

door opened and the one we were waiting for came out.

Hugging a large vessel to his side, it stood for a while (the light was beating right on its "face") and headed down the path, touching the leaves hanging down beside the path with its free hand. Could this creature, feeling its way along the path, have dug up the fields surrounding the settlement? Built the houses? Hunted? It was impossible to believe. And yet something had done it.

It continued moving, still touching the leaves.

Our lights followed it. They even showed its moving muscles. Everything we saw went against the grain of our earthly knowledge. It seemed to us that the creature must turn around any second in the direction of the blazing lights, scream in terror, and hide in the darkness. Our fingers were on the switches, and it was all we could do to take our hands off.

We looked on ahead to see where the path led, and we understood what the stranger was doing. It was on its way to a tiny lake, and the closer it got to it, the less certain its step became. The terrain was open here, and it bent down several times to touch the soil. It felt the edge of the shore with its foot, and when it was sure there was water in front of it, it lowered the vessel.

Now it had to get back. It started off correctly, but an animal flashed through the underbrush. We didn't get a good look at it, because it moved so quickly. But the hut's inhabitant sensed its presence, turned quickly and moved aside. Then it froze. It wasn't a man—it didn't look like one at all—but we saw its rib cage heaving and felt its terror, and for a second a bond grew up between us and this creature of eternal night. We even jumped up to run to its aid.

But it wasn't necessary; the predator left. The inhabitant got a better grip on the vessel, shook its head, crowned with "laurels"—actually, horns—and moved on. It didn't go toward the house. Its movements didn't change; it bent over, testing the soil, hampered by the water-filled vessel. But it wasn't walking toward the hut. It was headed away from the settlement, where the path ended at a ravine.

I heard my friends' heavy breathing, and I was as confused as they were.

Should we warn it of the danger? But what if it wanted to go to the cliff?

It was almost there. Very close to the edge. And then it sensed that something was wrong. It stayed in place, moving its head, as though trying to see something. Then it moved to the left. But the cliff was curved, and the only way to avoid it was by turning around completely. We waited to see what it would do. It was inches away from the drop. It froze.

"Back, back!" Irina couldn't restrain herself. As though he could hear the walkie-talkie.

It took a step. Into the void. Even as it fell, it did not drop the vessel of precious water. We heard a scream.

What we didn't want to believe was true. This world was blind, but it had gone blind recently.

"You know as well as I do that we can't do that," Zibella said.

"We have no alternative," Irina said.

We were standing over the alien's body, unsure what to do. We were at a dead end, thanks to a very reasonable regulation. To learn what disaster had befallen the planet we had to perform an autopsy on the lifeless body. But was it really lifeless? We couldn't determine that for sure without a thorough study of the higher forms of life on this planet, and we hadn't done that yet. And knowing nothing about its physiology, we could easily become murderers of the creature, who might be only unconscious.

But we couldn't waste time either.

"I recommend an introscopy of the internal organs," Irina said. "Right here."

Zibella replied as I would have in his place.

"Of course, that's the most reasonable course. But can you guarantee that the radiation will not harm him? Can you swear by the accuracy of such a diagnosis and determine without opening him up whether he is alive or not?"

Well, that's it, I thought. You can't guarantee a thing if the alien's organism doesn't resemble a human one. But, what the hell is this? I asked myself in dismay. We're making ourselves helpless, when we should be acting! If it were someone else other than Zibella . . .

"Yes," Irina said. "I can give you a complete guarantee."

I thought I had misheard her. But Irina's statement was nothing compared to Zibella's answer.

"Go ahead," he said.

And no more. Did Zibella know that Irina had stretched things a bit? Probably. Yet, even now Zibella had not deviated from the rule book. It said: "In a profoundly specialized situation the captain must rely on the opinions of the specialist." And so he did. And yet he did not absolve himself of responsibility. He could have said nothing or contradicted her; instead, he gave confirming orders.

Try to understand a man you think you know inside out. And there's nothing strange about it really, when you think about it. If the constant characteristic of our environment is contradiction (and it is), it would be silly to assume that there will ever be a race of people without unexpected personality contradictions.

"It's dead," Irina said, looking up from her apparatus.

We brought the body into the ship.

Our discovery only deepened the mystery. Study of the body revealed that the planet's inhabitants did have an organ of distance vision—that funny "laurel wreath" on the head. The wreath was their eyes, catching not light waves, naturally, since there were none, but the ultrashort electromagnetic waves emitted by the star that could penetrate the atmosphere.

Their radio sun, in our terms, barely glimmered in the sky. But for them, obviously, the murky world wasn't at all murky, since evolution had created a fantastically sensitive receptor organ. Thanks to their antennae-horns they could probably, just like us, enjoy sunsets, the colors of vegetation, the ripples and shimmers of the sea, everything that constitutes the visual world, even if that world was one of reflected radio waves, which we humans could not imagine.

That's the way it had been until they had gone blind.

Externally there was nothing wrong with the antennae; they simply did not function, and we could not understand why not.

Two explanations seemed likely. A sudden epidemic. And another one. We would not be blinded if our sun suddenly burst into light twice as intense as before because we have eyelids. But they didn't have any, nor did they need them, because the penetrating power of ultrashort waves is much less than that of light.

Wonderful theories, but they were worthless. What epidemic could have affected all the planet's inhabitants so quickly? A sudden increase in the radio brightness of the star, of course, could have created that effect, but our measurements indicated that at least during our stay the star behaved normally.

We argued for six hours or so and broke up the meeting feeling groggy. The answer was near, we all sensed that. Our confusion was frustrating; we wanted to treat our brains the way you do a malfunctioning machine—by giving it a good sock.

I couldn't sleep, and I suspect the others couldn't either. As soon as I shut my eyes, I saw the little figure frozen on the edge of the cliff. I could hear its scream. I preferred to keep my eyes open, even though the room was completely dark. As dark as the planet. No, this won't do, I thought. We won't get anywhere if we keep thinking in earth terms.

How do we get around that? Our whole way of thinking, our psychology, was so inexorably tied to Earth that it was impossible to get away. Well, that wasn't precisely true. We'd been on several planets, and I guess we could get away from earthly preconceptions somewhat. Not completely, but we can. But the concepts related to the sun—those are hard to lose. Wherever we go, we surround ourselves with light, with the atmosphere of the sun's rays. And there's nothing you can do about it. We know that there are other forms of light; we've created and used instruments that see in other ways than we do, but even in using them we reduced their data to visual images or abstract symbols. Reason is our guide, but the eye is its most trusted counselor. Try replacing it with a radio eye. You can do that with a machine, but not with a human.

That was an idea! Send down a robot with a radio eye of the same capabilities and sensitivity and see what happened to it!

I turned on the light excitedly. As always after the dark, for a few seconds all I saw was the flat, painfully bright outlines of objects. And that's what happened on the planet, I thought. An explosion that singed the eye, and then the blindness and murkiness. The poor things didn't have eyelids.

My heart was beating wildly. We had been looking for an explosion, because all our experience insisted that only an explosion could blind. But what if we should be looking for something else? We're the ones who can close our lids, not they. The level of radiation coming from the star, which we thought was normal because of its stability, might not be normal for them at all. Could that be it?

It explained everything.

It explained nothing! On earth, even if the sun shone once in a million years for a month or two at an intensity that was ten times higher than usual, evolution would account for it somehow. All the more here. It just couldn't be that the star had always shone steadily and then had gone berserk just as we got there. Of course, it was possible, but it was too much of a coincidence.

And yet there was something in it—in the coincidence, as though our arrival, either in how we approached or how we . . .

Without dressing, I rushed into the engine room. Leo was still there and looked startled, but I didn't give him a chance to say anything.

"What range are our locators working in?"

"I'll check. Why?"

"You don't know?"

"You think I can remember with all this other stuff going on? The computers take care of it. Why?"

But I had already read the meters myself.

"Leo, I beg you, what is the approximate intensity of the locators on the surface? Can you give me the order of magnitude?

He told me. He still didn't understand. Everything was swimming before my eyes.

Our computer had picked the frequencies for which the atmosphere was most transparent and which were for that reason the "life light" on the planet. But our equipment was less sensitive than the inhabitant's "eyes," and we wanted to see as well as possible. And so the locators burst into blinding light.

We had blinded this world, for we had been certain that the properties of human physiology were our business and no one else's.

Leo was saying something, but I didn't hear him. I saw the black planet where we would have to spend many long years salvaging what could still be saved. The thought of the depressing hell that awaited us, strangely enough, brought me relief.

# The Inexorable Finger of Fate

ANDREI SEMYONOVICH MILOVIDOV's favorite pleasures were an easy chair, coffee with oatmeal cookies, and quiet music in the evening. This does not mean, however, that his actions resembled the measured rhythm of a machine. Such a man dwells only in the imagination. The real Milovidov, sitting that evening quietly in front of his radio, got up and fiddled with the reception dial.

Wow, bzzz, sprrrt, pshshhh!

The sound of a dozen stations, howling, whistling, and crackling, blended into a horrible din. The cacophony, however, amused Milovidov, and he repeated his experiment, a rather suspicious one from a psychiatric point of view.

Wow, bzzz, sprrrt, pshshhh!

"Today, July 24, our city is host for the football team from . . ."

The announcer's bored voice went on, and Milovidov was about to look for a music station, when he asked himself:

"Isn't today the 23rd?"

It was the 23rd. As a bank teller, he knew that for sure, because the wrong date on a financial transaction could cause all kinds of unpleasantness, and he had to keep a sharp eye on his customers—it was amazing how careless people were with dates!

The announcer again mentioned the day's date as being the 24th, and Milovidov went on listening to the report on the progress of the hay harvest, because he was intrigued by the stubborn repetition of the same mistake. It was shocking—yes, yes, shocking!—to be so slipshod about one's duties. And trains are always late, too, Milovidov thought. He waited to see what would happen next.

Next came news on fish hatcheries, the new traffic regulations, the shipment of imported men's suits in the department store, and a story about a robbery at the bank on Aprelsky Street. The bank in which Milovidov worked.

"And now the weather. Tomorrow, July 25th, we expect partly cloudy skies in our area . . ."

The voice slowly faded away, as though its owner were disappearing into another world. Milovidov anxiously twirled his dial, but he couldn't get the voice back. There was just a hiss and nothing else.

Milovidov glanced at his watch. It was eight-forty-five, and he knew definitely that the local station didn't broadcast at all at that time of night.

And Milovidov felt unwell. His armchair began sinking and rising like a balloon.

On the morning of the 24th the small bank on Aprelsky Street opened as usual at nine o'clock. Milovidov, as usual, breathed on his glasses, wiped them with his handkerchief, and got ready to accept and hand out money. If that newscast was to be believed, today that money would be taken away from them, perhaps by force of arms. Even definitely by force of arms.

Milovidov's mind worked like a grain mill. He had dismissed the idea of calling the police last night, for reasons obvious to any normal person. For the same reason he couldn't talk to his fellow cashiers. The more he thought, the more hopeless the situation seemed. Can knowledge of the future change the future? And if it can, how? And what should he do? He found no anwers.

His hands continued to operate independently of his head—he counted, recounted, gave out, took in, noted, signed, and the external world beyond his glass partition looked like a strange aquarium filled with ever-changing faces that flashed by, moved their lips, and stuck to the glass. They changed in rhythm to the flash of the bills that his agile fingers handled. Denominations with denominations, pictures aligned.

How could people not know that money must be stacked a certain way? All went on without his being conscious of it, while he brooded.

Suppose he could find out the future. What could he change, if his knowledge was limited to the very event he wanted to eliminate? If he managed to prevent that event from happening, that would mean that it would not happen. Then how could he have found out about it? Or are there several futures?

"They have some new imported stuff at the store," the comptroller told him during a break.

"Yes?" Milovidov got flustered. "How do you know?"

"A friend of mine who's a saleslady whispered it to me on the bus. They say it's only men's suits. I guess I should run over at lunch."

"Do they have sweaters?" the supervisor asked over Milovidov's head.

Two weak women, Milovidov thought glumly. And it's a whole block to the traffic cop.

"Right, Andrei Semyonovich?"

"Huh?"

"You seem awfully pale, dearie. Sick?"

"No, no, everything's fine."

"I think that a gray suit would look better on you."

"Really?"

Milovidov looked at his jacket's worn cuffs and suddenly, clearly, nightmarishly, imagined a spreading bloodstain where his pocket was. The report had said nothing about victims, but that didn't mean that there weren't going to be any!

He dropped a ten and it slid to the floor, something that hadn't happened to Milovidov in a long time. Luckily, the supervisor was called away, and she forgot about her question.

Milovidov could think of nothing but the possibility of death. His bank had never been robbed—there hadn't been a robbery in the entire city in the last ten years—but he knew that there were victims during robberies, and most often they were tellers. But what could he do?

He finally realized that whatever the mutability of the future was, shooting was not necessarily a part of it, since there had been no mention of it in the broadcast. That meant that within its limits he could vary his future.

The logic was not impeccable, but when an unavoidable disaster hovers over a man, he has no time for logic. Strange, but he had no doubts now that the broadcast had come from the future. Actually, there was nothing incredible about it: Milovidov believed completely in what he read, and many recent popular science articles had convinced him that science could do anything.

The closer the hands on the clock got to noon, the stronger was the grip of the fear that engulfed Andrei Semyonovich. It wasn't a rational fear, when the brain works feverishly to find a way out, but an animal fear that made him cold inside, made him want to run. The report had said that the robbery had taken place around midday, and it was now around eleven.

It'll happen in an hour, maybe less, he thought.

"I have to go to a meeting," the supervisor said, hanging up the phone. "It's all right—there aren't too many customers right now, you can manage without me. I'll be back by two."

"What should I do if they bring deposits?" the comptroller asked.

"You're in charge, dearie. There's nothing to it. You've done it before."

"She's always in meetings, and we do all the work," the comptroller grumbled, as the door slammed shut behind the supervisor.

She was obviously expecting sympathy from Milovidov, and he always gave it to her. It was automatic, a habit like brushing his teeth. He managed to squeeze out a sympathetic "Humph."

Eleven-thirty. Andrei Milovidov had lost his interest in the people who came up to his window a long time ago. Hands—what he usually saw was hands, handing him money, taking it. Once in a while, when he was really busy or it was close to closing time, he would get angry if the hands were clumsy or put the money too far away so that he had to reach for it. But when it was quiet he might amuse himself by tallying how many people had dirty fingernails. He also classified hands by how they handled money—grabbing it, holding it tenderly, or indifferently, or disdainfully. In general, he did not like hands that took money, because that meant he had to hand it to them. There were reasons for this dislike. The more money in the bank, the greater the profits. And that could mean a bonus. But that wasn't the main reason. Milovidov liked money as a craftsman likes his tools, a driver his car, a writer his pen. That's why he liked hands that turned in money, and he sympathized with them as they parted with money and unconsciously hesitated for a fraction of a second—that brief moment was an eloquent poem for Milovidov. And spreading and smoothing out crumpled bills was a pleasure, too, like combing someone's unkempt children.

But now he was looking at money with horror. It was treachery on their part—risking his life. Yes, treachery! He hadn't done anyone any harm, he was always peaceful and quiet, so why? Why him?

A teller's life is full of hidden anxieties, because he is responsible for every penny that comes into his hands, and a mistake in calculation may have far-reaching repercussions. Milovidov couldn't admit this even to himself, but there lived a constant and ancient fear in his heart, as corrosive as rust. Fear that he had learned to hide from himself. A fear that led to his submission to statutes and regulations, the desire for as many of them as possible, because they defined the limits of his actions, and therefore limited the possibility of a mistake. That was sheer self-delusion. His whole manner was shaped and formed by this fear, and now he felt naked, helpless, because there was nothing standing between him and impending doom—no counters, no regulations, no rules. Perhaps that was how a turtle felt pulled out of its shell. A turtle that knew it was about to be pulled out of its shell.

Now Milovidov watched the faces that flickered in front of his window, trying to guess which of them would look at him ruthlessly. There hadn't been a ruthless face yet, just ordinary faces—tired, friendly, worried, bored. The one he was waiting for and pictured clearly had not appeared yet.

He kept making disjointed plans. The signal button—could he set it off by accident? Better a scene, than . . . He was about to do it. But he couldn't. He had just enough energy left for the customary, automatic motions, and he made them, hoping they would create a magic circle around him, as though as long as he maintained the prescribed order, that order would keep disaster at bay. Order was like walls, like fortress walls. He couldn't breach them.

He thought about disappearing into the bathroom when it was almost noon. But he was too chivalrous to abandon a woman. And how could he guess the right time? Like a rabbit in a cobra's gaze, he could no longer think clearly. It would come, and he was resigned. And, without thinking about it, he knew what he would do.

Externally he continued working as before.

Maybe it was that man . . . or that one . . . no, not him.

The faces moved behind the glass, looking at him as though from another world.

Noon.

"Are you sick?" the comptroller asked him.

What's she talking about?

"Oh . . . it's nothing. I have a chill," he said, wiping away the cold sweat.

"It's the weather, all these changes. You'd better take care of yourself."

"I'm all right."

He'd take care of himself. Of course he would.

Five after twelve. Ten after.

And then a happy thought came to him. The broadcast was from a different year! Of course! Why had he assumed that it was from this year? Naturally, it was from some other year.

Milovidov experienced bliss, as if he had returned to his youth, when he had viewed all elderly people with superiority, sure that he had his whole life in front of him to do with as he would, and they had their lives behind them. He would do better! The cramped office with its fake wood-paneled walls, the daylight behind the dusty window, the counters polished by many elbows, the crack in the ceiling that they had been promising to fix for months—everything seemed so sweet.

There was no one on the other side of the glass partition; the last customer had made a transaction and left. These inexplicable breaks happened almost every day, and the emptiness was perfectly in tune with Milovidov's spring mood.

The mood disappeared suddenly, blown away by a cold wind. If someone was waiting for the right moment, what could be better than when the two of them were alone in the bank?

"Andrei Semyonovich, I'll only be gone a minute, while there's no one here. I'll be right back."

Milovidov did not reply. It was clear and inevitable. It was all leading up to it. First the supervisor. Now the comptroller. Why shouldn't she go when no one was there, if she really had to go? And now it had to happen, right now when he was alone and it was quiet and empty in the room. *He* would appear.

Milovidov recognized *him* when he came up to the door. Actually, there were two of them. That's the way it should have been, two, or maybe even three.

It was all happening just the way his imagination had pictured it. A fellow with a cap lowered over his eyes looked around without turning his head, and slowly headed straight for Milovidov's window. His partner was leaning against the wall by the exit, hands in pockets, staring at the street with a look of total disinterest.

The face of the man who came up to the window was familiar too. His eyes, murky as a sunrise, looked at him ruthlessly. There was no anger, no frenzy, no human feelings at all in them. And the eyes were getting closer.

"Well, pal, alone guarding the mint, huh?" His winy breath reached Milovidov. "You'll have to cough up."

Milovidov was waiting for a gun muzzle in his face, but the guy pulled a lottery ticket from his pocket. His partner shifted positions at the door. He was tense, ready to leap.

Milovidov took the ticket, understanding nothing, seeing nothing, except the murky eyes that were boring into him. A feverish idea penetrated his fear-frozen brain: This was only a diversion.

His extended hand still held the ticket.

"Well, so?" the bandit asked without any intonation. "Do we have to wait all day?"

"Hurry it up," the man by the door said hoarsely.

Milovidov saw him reach slowly for his pocket.

"Right away."

Not hearing his own voice, he put down the ticket, opened the drawer and took out stack after stack of bills. Even at that moment he was functioning with the same precision with which he always handed out withdrawals, only faster and without counting.

The guy by the window gathered up the pile, and something in his face changed. Milovidov didn't catch what it was.

"Fantastic," he said, shoving the money into his pockets and heading for the door.

His pal froze with a cigarette in one hand and matches in the other.

"That's really something!" he gasped. "How . . ."

"I don't know. I thought it was a ruble win," the murky-eyed guy shrugged. "Let's go."

When they were out on the street, Milovidov desperately pushed the alarm, not fully understanding it all, but sensing that something irrevocable had happened.

# A Place in Memory

"ARE YOU THE DIRECTOR of the Memorial?"

I looked up and saw a man so old that he seemed flat. His no-iron suit hung in folds on him and moved in a time lapse after his body moved, as though considering announcing its total independence of him.

"At your service! Take a seat."

He lowered himself into the armchair.

The old man looked at me for a couple of minutes. He had small eyes under thinning gray brows, and they were of such a blank gray color that I felt inexplicably uneasy.

"So, I'm speaking with the director," he said in confirmation. "I must call your attention to the fact that the institution you direct is mismanaged."

He paused, waiting for something, the expected reaction from me. But I went on listening calmly.

"So," he continued, his voice whiny. "Your Memorial Center approached me, as it should have, to dictate my memoirs. I treated the matter with all due seriousness, because I appreciate the value of the experience of the older generation, the value of the observations and realizations we've made. Of course, I am a simple man, but even my life was filled with the struggle for the glorious and advanced idea that is the main goal, which, in its turn . . . "

In the fifth minute of his monologue the chair I was sitting in developed hard spots that I had never noticed before. And I wanted to look out the window, at the birds skimming and flitting. . . .

" . . . the value of the Memorial Center lies in the fact that it is the receptor of the experience that . . . Every man has the right, which cannot be overlooked without damaging society as a whole, and therefore the workers and staff of the Memorial and the machines they operate must treat them with all responsibility . . . "

I nodded docilely. There was no point in correcting him. The Memorial Center really was a major advance in cybernetics, but certainly not a complete collection of the memoirs of everyone and his brother. Yes, any man, whatever his age, could tune in to our channel and relate the story of his life, with all the minutiae so dear to his heart (anonymity is guaranteed by law). We particularly tried to get the old people, if they were not nagging us themselves. A million destinies, a million unrepeatable acts, thoughts, and feelings, all the personal things that used to disappear with death were now gathered and preserved, lived forever, and this wealth was priceless. It was not important that in the memoirs the truth was often changed or embellished; both what had happened and what had been invented were important—both were part of life! The important thing was not to confuse the two—and that's why we had the special filter systems that sorted and distinguished. Here you are, sociologist, teacher, historian, or psychologist, here you have a million nameless, confidential tapes, about what a man felt and thought, how he acted in one situation or another. Dip in, reason out, formulate rules. Today's progress in these sciences could not have been made without our center. Nor our new flowering of literature. How many people could a writer of the past have met, how many secrets could his eye uncover? Now the souls of people who were no more were open to him.

But what had we done wrong to this old man?

" . . . based on what I've said, I decided to find out how many memory cells my story took. And what do you think I found out? Are you interested in the result?"

The old man's voice went up in pitch. Something like reinforced concrete crept into his voice—an inviolate belief in his rightness. Rightness and rights.

"So," he said, anger and suspicion in his eye, "one ugly fact came to light. Very ugly. The information service gave me a report which states that my memoirs were assigned," he waited a second, "zero cells!"

He waited for the full weight of his statement to sink in, and then continued with excitement.

"Zero cells, do you hear? That is, nothing! How could that be possible? How am I supposed to interpret this?"

There was nothing to interpret; it was all perfectly clear to me. The fact that the machine had excerpted nothing from his tale meant only one thing: his story was a fake. There was nothing personal, unique, fresh in it; it was only banality, which the machine rejected. It was all garbage, without a single original thought, honest emotion, or even new fact.

I had to get out of it—quickly and carefully, without upsetting the old man.

"That's shocking!" I exclaimed, grabbing the intercom. "You're right, you're absolutely right!"

"I know that," he said sententiously.

My remaining doubts were settled. Not now nor ever did he once think his memoirs might be totally useless drivel. He was worried only that an unjust mistake had been made, depriving humanity of his precious memoirs. That's all! Poor fool.

I made believe I was checking and clearing up something that needed no clarification. Meanwhile he spoke passionately.

"Man—that has a proud ring to it!" he said, raising his finger to make his point. "Marvelous words that everyone should keep in mind, particularly you, you who deal with preserving spiritual treasures. Any life lived honestly and responsibly, even if it is a modest one, is worthy of respect and memory. It is not I who says this, but society, for whose sake humble workers such as I worked unstintingly . . . "

He was right. There are no uninteresting fates, and each man takes away the universe when he dies. But I couldn't tell him this. I couldn't tell him that his speech, and therefore his thinking, was ossified, that he had told his life, habitually deleting "everything irrelevant," everything which might have been slightly original. And he had once had it, to be sure—his memory still contained something unique—but it was hopeless to knock and call for it now. It was long buried, sealed, and forgotten.

"So there you are, it was a mistake," I said, hanging up. "A minor technical error; I'm afraid they still happen. We ask your forgiveness, we will take all steps—"

"Will you tape them again?"

"Naturally! Immediately, if you so desire."

"Yes. Even though it does mean a new depletion of time and strength, which thanks to your sloppiness . . . "

I said nothing, trying to look profoundly abashed. It was hard; I'm no actor. I hate lying, but there was no other way as far as I could see. The truth would anger and hurt him, and he wouldn't believe it, taking it for hostility or calumny. And what if he did believe it? No, anything but that! To realize at the end of your life that you never thought for yourself and had only secondhand feelings, that you never gave people anything of your own, and perhaps, even worse than that, you were in the way, like an obsolete regulation. No, no! Why ruin the old man's last years?

Luckily, realization did not threaten him. Finishing his sermon, he got up, and so did I, to see him out. But he stopped in the center of the rug and began talking again. I listened, feeling my facial muscles turn to wood.

The hardest part was ahead. I had to figure out a way to fool him when he checked up again (and he would!) to see how many cells his memoirs took up. I don't know what I would have given to fill up those memory cells. But that would not happen. Zero—it would be zero again. Because the machine did everything it could the first time. And it can do a lot. It doesn't merely record a story; it can, like the best interviewer, make a reluctant person open up, and if it hadn't managed to come up with even a grain of necessary information, then it was hopeless.

"I was a contemporary of Gagarin's!" he announced, standing on my threshold. "I remember it all as though it were yesterday. I was the contemporary of great construction projects! I was there. I've been . . ."

Precisely. He had been.

When the door finally shut behind him, I fell exhausted in my chair. And then I thought, when it came my turn to tell my life story, would I have the nerve to find out how many cells I was allotted?

No. Never.

# Intelligence Test

PETER KEPT PROCRASTINATING, even though he knew he should go right in without hesitation, wake up Ev, if he was sleeping, and confess that he, engineer and first-class crewman Peter Fanney, had seen a ghost.

It had happened in one of those distant compartments where the steady vibration was a reminder of the proximity of the annihilators of space and time. A force that could destroy a small planet was confined next to the compartment, and his senses were naturally heightened in the dim, narrow, trembling passageways.

Peter felt the way he always did, however. He probably would have been surprised to discover that he, the master of this monstrous machine, harbored the same anxieties that his distant ancestors experienced when nature manifested itself in blinding bolts of lightning or in the menacing smell of a predator along the path.

He was finishing up his rounds, when he was rooted to the spot by a quiet and totally impossible cough.

He turned.

No one, nothing. An empty corridor, the dull glow of the enamel on the walls, and the serpentine shadows of cables and pipes. And the physical sensation, like a spiderweb stuck to his face, of someone's gaze on him.

"Oleg, is that you?" Peter called out tensely.

The hall was silent. Peter was alone, completely alone in the bowels of the smoothly functioning machine.

A second later Peter realized the inappropriateness, even the shamefulness, of his position, and he stepped resolutely toward the sound, shifting the satchel with the testers closer to his body, as though to tell himself that he was equal to any coughing, sneezing, or giggling problem.

But he hadn't taken two steps when something raced away from the wall, something so fast and shapeless that his memory recorded only a ball of black smoke that, as it disappeared around the corner, gleamed at him with two blood-red eyes.

By the time Peter's weakened legs had carried him out on the platform where the thing had gone, there was nothing in either direction, only the two corridors, filled with vibration, mirroring each other infinitely. Panting, Peter raced down both corridors, and the distance separating him from the inhabited parts of the starship seemed terrifyingly vast.

The explanation seemed obvious. It had happened in the past, when the burden of an extended flight took its toll on the nerves of the crew, but as far as Peter could remember, no one had ever seen a ghost before.

That made his position worse. He was obliged to report what had happened to him to the doctor—that is, to old man Ev—and it was easy to predict what would happen after that.

He was inexpressibly sorry for himself. It was unfair, unfair, unfair! Why him? Why? And anyway, how could it have happened? After all, he felt no worse than usual.

"Ev, are you asleep?" he asked quietly by the open door.

Stupid question. Naturally at this late hour the chief surgeon and biologist was sleeping, exhausted from the hard days of work on Bissera. Maybe he shouldn't be waking him just then?

Peter rubbed his chin, thinking. He was required to see the doctor, that was true. He had to tell him everything that happened, yes. But there was a difference between reporting now and a little later. A big difference! His reactions were probably out of kilter now. After a little rest and sleep, maybe . . .

He decided. Peter Fanney walked steadily to his bunk, undressed, and went to bed. He wasn't shaking anymore. It was quiet in the room. There was nothing here to remind him of the speed with which the starship, racing to Earth, was cutting through space.

The starship, on board of which a man had seen a ghost—which, of course, could not have happened.

A few minutes later, Peter was asleep. A good spaceman, Peter had nerves of steel.

But he slept badly. Back on earth, where he found himself, he was lying in a hammock, which immediately turned into a spiderweb, and his heart was in his throat, because the spider was bound to appear any second. Peter knew that it was nearby, for he could feel the touch of its hairy legs, but he couldn't move, and the worst part was that the spider was invisible. Then, still in the spiderweb, Peter was looking into a microscope, and this, he knew, was his last chance to pass the test on which everything depended. The microscope, however, instead of revealing the spider, showed him Ev's mustache, his audacious red mustache, and Peter kept thinking desperately that this couldn't be the final exam, even though he knew that it was. With great effort he threw off the blasted microscope to try a new one. The microscope fell, rolling like a ball, and the ball shone with an icy fire, getting bigger, and Peter's heart contracted, for this was no longer a ball, but a concentrated neutron star. "So, this is how galaxies are born," flashed through his horror-struck brain.

A noise ended Peter's nightmare. He jumped up, listening. His heart was beating wildly, but reality was dispelling the dream's power. There was a distinct banging and what sounded like screams. Somewhere close. Maybe in the toilet, which was next door. Peter ran into the hall. He was right: someone was cursing and banging on the locked bathroom door. Peter pulled at the door, and Oleg fell out of the toilet like a cat out of a bag.

"Whose little joke was that?" he demanded, without giving Peter a chance to think. "Some joke! Humor on the amoeba level, a caveman's bathroom prank!"

"Did they have bathrooms then?" Peter asked, stunned.

The question was so ridiculous that they stopped and stared at each other.

"When will we be able to get some sleep around here?" a grumpy voice asked. A door creaked, and Ev's face, blinking and squinting, popped into the hallway. "What's going on?"

He looked at the two undressed cosmonauts.

"Oleg was locked in here," Peter mumbled in confusion.

"I see. Has anyone been burned in the reactor yet? It seems like the right time," Ev said.

"The fact remains that the door was locked by someone who was giggling," Oleg barked. "I would like to know—"

"The deep secret of a bizarre mystery." Ev nodded. "Is this a starship or what?"

"It could have been a malfunctioning cyber-robot." Peter suggested.

"Aha!" Ev's eyes were glistening. "Wrapped in galactic darkness, the metal monster stealthily crept up to the sleeping cosmonaut's slippers. By the way, Peter, what did you do to your slippers?"

"To what?"

They all looked down at Peter's feet. His purple-spotted slippers were full of holes.

"The end of the world," Oleg sighed. "And chock full of practical jokers."

"Really, Peter, what did you do to them?"

"Ev." Peter's voice broke. "I have to talk to you, Ev."

"Nonsense!" Ev discarded the miogram tape. It got caught on the tuner and hung swaying in the air. "What ghost? The diagnosis unit maintains that you are well, and I agree with that contraption."

"I assure you—"

"Extreme nervous agitation, and nothing more. All your basal reactions—"

"What about the slippers?"

"What about the slippers? What do they have to do with this? So you burned them with something."

"What?"

"Fruit cocktail!" Ev shouted. "Cabbage soup! What are you trying to prove? Chock full of jokers, as Oleg said. And they're all making jokes. Wake you up in the middle of the night . . . ghosts of murder victims, giggling, locking people in the toilet . . . Just wait, I'm going to give you one hell of a tranquilizer."

He reached over to the desk, but didn't pick up the ampule. Anton Ramsey stood in the doorway. Stood and stared at him in a way that made Peter want to cut out immediately.

"So," the captain said, walking toward Ev. "I have a small question for you, as our biologist and medical officer. Can a mouse, say, disappear into the fourth dimension?"

"Anton," Ev asked, his eyes growing round, "have you signed up in the jokers' brigade as well?"

"Jokers? I'm asking you: where are the animals?"

"Animals?"

"Yes, animals!"

"From Bissera?"

"From Bissera."

"Where they're supposed to be. Why?"

"Nothing. They're not there, that's all."

"Not there? What do you mean?"

"That's what I'd like to find out."

"But that's impossible."

"That's right."

"Anton, it's impossible!! What a cheap trick!"

Ev turned to Peter, as though inviting him to share his irritation, then looked up at the captain again—and the color drained from his face.

Yes, thought Peter, looking over Ev's shoulder at the vitalization boxes, if someone has gone mad, at least it's not me. This beats everything!

All along the length of the room lay small and large transparent sarcophaguses, which had controlled artificial environments to keep the specimens from Bissera in suspended animation. At least a third of the sarcophaguses were empty. Each had an impressively large hole burned in it.

The control monitor, as though in mockery, showered green lights, meaning corrective work on the vitalization computer. Too late and rather huffily, the signals monitoring life systems blinked, with nothing left to monitor.

"And how do you expect me to explain this?"

There was no answer. Ev was so pale that his reddish mustache seemed flame-red.

"Don't worry," the captain said, gently touching his shoulder. "If I'm not mistaken, the stagers, asphetes, trojans, katushs, and those, um . . ."

"Missandras," Ev whispered.

" . . . missandras are gone. The pseudosnakes are still here. Does that give you a clue?"

Ev shook his head.

"The vitalization level of dormancy is maintained in all the hermetically sealed bells at a median level, optimal for the whole group." He spoke in a monotone, delivering a memorized lesson. "It follows that there is the possibility of a particular specimen needing a higher level and waking up. But in that case, the computer would immediately increase the level—which it did. I don't understand a thing. The bells could be burned through like that only with a spark discharge!"

"Maybe one of the creatures—" the captain began, but Ev shook his head desperately.

"I saw one of them on the ship," Peter said suddenly.

They turned to him in unison. He briefly explained about his ghost.

"That must have been a katush," Ev said slowly.

"No," Peter countered. "I know what a katush looks like. This was something else."

"Doesn't matter," the captain said softly. "So, Ev, there's no explanation that you can offer?"

"None."

"All right, we'll function without an explanation. I'm putting us on red alert."

At the entrance to the control room, Ev took the captain's elbow.

"I have an explanation. I didn't want to mention it in front of Peter."

"Well?" Ev felt the captain's muscles tighten.

"Captain, the animals could not have escaped on their own. That's ruled out. They were let out, Anton."

"Do you realize what you're saying?"

"That's why I insist on a general examination of the crew."

The captain wiped the sweat from his brow.

"Whom do you suspect?" he asked.

"If I hadn't just examined him, I would have said Peter. But it's not Peter. I don't want to think about it, but someone did lock in Oleg. And someone poured acid over Peter's slippers."

"Nevertheless, I will not give permission for a general examination," the captain said firmly.

"But—"

"Ev, you don't put out a fire by shouting, 'There's an arsonist among us!' "

Meanwhile, Peter, at his post, was examining his left arm in disbelief. He had just noticed a dot, the kind you have after an injection, where his vein showed blue under the skin.

"That's strange! But I guess I should tell them."

At first everyone was sure that catching a few dumb animals would be no problem, but they were weaned of that illusion fast enough. The living space of the starship took up several square kilometers, and it had never occurred to the builders that the ship might become a hunting field. Once or twice, however, they did manage to flush some creature, which would immediately fly up above their heads into the tangle of decks, elevators, and catwalks. Since the only flying Bissera specimen was the missandra, then naturally that had to be the missandra. But where were the others?

The suggestion to program the cyber-robots to hunt the animals was immediately rejected by Ev—he knew that regular robots could not be pitted against protein, matter related to humans. The biological robots he had used to round up specimens on Bissera were useless in the ship's cramped passages.

The more Ev thought about it, the less he liked it. The possibility that a madman had opened the vitalization chambers seemed likely enough. But assuming that someone had freed the animals, what then? Bissera's atmosphere did not resemble earth's. How were they breathing? And they were breathing, that was a fact.

He finally shared his thoughts with the captain.

"What is this?" Ramsey demanded. "You've studied them and you don't even know what they can breathe and what they can't?"

"You're justified in reproaching me, Anton. But who was it who cut back on the biological program? I know, I know, there was an emergency call from earth, we're needed—desperately, as usual—in the opposite quadrant of the galaxy. What do I care? What could I do in the remaining time? This is so typical! We're always in a rush, one star today, another tomorrow, hurry hurry, more work than we can handle, no time to stop and think. Don't think I'm trying to shift the blame from myself, but . . ."

"We're in a hurry, that's true. Otherwise we might not be traveling to the stars today. But how are they adapting to our atmosphere?"

"Highly flexible metabolism, I suppose. It's really very flexible."

"All right, you can check it out after we've caught them. What's this idea you have for traps?"

They discussed new tactics. They were constantly interrupted by members of the search party. "Captain, Peter's uncovered tracks left by invisible animals."

Peter interrupted the transmission: "I've been telling you for a long time that we don't have enough robots. They can't manage to do all the vacuuming."

"All right, all right," came the sarcastic reply. "We close our eyes to the situation, but who'll close the eyes of the commission?"

"Don't laugh, you guys, that's not dust. It's cigarette ashes. I'm telling you the mechanics are sneaking smokes."

"It's not the mechanics at all. It's Ev's animals. If they can escape, why can't they smoke?"

The captain turned off the speaker.

He was annoyed. He wasn't too worried by the animals—where could they go?—but the thought of a madman on board . . .The order to stay in pairs had been accepted with surprised shrugs. That was all right, he thought, let them shrug, as long as no one guesses the reason. The captain was responsible for everything that happened, that's the way it always was and always would be, no matter what distances man conquered, and that was the only way to live for Ramsey—to worry about everything, foresee everything, and be on top of every situation. He was always on the lookout for blind chance, but this time, blind chance had caught him unaware. Was this a warning that he was petering out? The captain was furious. No, no, he would prove he wasn't slipping!

Prove to whom? The animals? The situation? Himself?

Ramsey controlled himself, and Ev had noticed nothing.

"Maybe this plan will get better results," he said coldly, examining the blueprint. "You explain to the technicians what you want. I'll get the group together."

"It wouldn't be bad to eat something, either. Personally, after all these hassles, I could eat a fried missandra."

Leaving the control room, Ev noticed Peter waiting for him.

"Here," Peter said, showing him the mark on his wrist. "You can laugh if you want, but I swear, I didn't give myself the shot."

Ev took a look and his skin crawled.

The lunch started out with high spirits, but the jokes soon stopped because the captain was in such a bad mood.

"What's with him?" Oleg whispered. "So the animals are running all over the place."

"Yeah, but now he'll be the laughingstock of the galaxy," his neighbor replied.

"I think they'll be laughing at Ev."

"We're all going to get it. Listen, haven't the girls overdone it with the perfume today?"

"Oh, you noticed it too?"

"A dead man would notice."

The captain looked up.

"Musa!"

"Yessir."

"What's wrong with the ventilation system? Where's that smell coming from?"

"As I understand it, sir, our feminine companions—"

A noisy protest cut him off.

"That's not perfume!"

"Enough!" It was very quiet. "Air control, immediately check . . ."

The captain didn't finish, because there was suddenly such a disgusting odor in the room that everyone jumped up, scattering chairs over the floor, and the siren went off.

Ev and Ramsey were sitting back to back to monitor all the screens hurriedly set up in the control room. They were still wearing gas masks, even though the stink had disappeared as quickly as it had appeared, created by a foul-smelling but harmless mixture of hydrogen sulfide and hydrogen bromide.

The cameras were set up at every major intersection on the ship, and primitive but effective traps were suspended from the ceiling. They just had to sit and wait until one of the escapees showed up on the screen.

Minutes passed and nothing happened. The speaker was silent—no one was in the mood for jokes. They were all behind locked doors, clutching weapons, guarding the ship's vital points and waiting. No one could say for what.

"Finally!"

Ev pushed a button.

The creature on the screen froze, as though sensing the trap. It was too late—it was struggling in the pliant silicete net.

"Got him!" the captain rejoiced.

"Uh-huh. I'd like to know what."

"What do you mean? That's the asphete."

"A winged asphete."

"Winged?"

Yes, the animal struggling in the net had wings. Like a missandra. And six extremities. Like an asphete. And a tubular naked tail, like no animal at all.

"Ev," the captain pleaded. "You're a biologist, Ev. You're the one who trapped them. Explain them!"

Ev's face was deathly pale.

"Ev!" the captain shook him by the shoulder.

"Look!"

The animal lay on the floor in a dark ball, and only its tubular tail twitched slightly. No, it wasn't twitching. The captain's jaw dropped. It was slowly, surely dividing in two. The tail was turning into something like a pair of scissors, and the blades were very sharp. They clamped onto a few links of the net.

But that's silicete, the captain thought.

The tail dropped the net—it hadn't given. Now the tail was changing color—from brown to steel gray. It opened again, and it was obvious that its blades were getting shorter. The men shuddered when they heard the crunch of silicete. A few snips of the pliant, doubled cutting tail, and the creature shook off the remains of the net, and the screen was empty.

"Well," Ev said, turning to the captain. "You can beat me. I was such an idiot! I deserve it."

"You . . . understood?"

"It's so clear. They reshape their bodies!" Ev said.

"I saw that. I mean, we both observed it. But damned if I understood a thing!"

"Listen," Ev spoke quickly. "There are no asphetes, missandras, and the rest of the lot. They were all the same thing. A completely different type of evolution. What was I thinking about before? This is phenomenal!"

"And over my head," the captain added. "We've got to do something."

"You have to understand, and you will. Sit down. On earth a wolf is always a wolf, a partridge is always a partridge, and an amoeba is always an amoeba. But their bodies are basically made of the same cells, and their biochemistry is similar. They are part of a whole. Like a pitcher, glass, mirror—"

"Mirror?"

"Yes, they're all glass. Earth evolution splintered a single biological entity into thousands of independent forms. And here the forms are mutable. An elephant on Bissera can become a whale or a herd of rabbits, because they are all the same thing. An organism that can transform its body as it wants into anything it wants. On the command of the nervous system."

"On command?"

"Precisely. On earth, biological matter is shaped in one form or another by external circumstances. Slowly, inevitably, they become dissimilar forms. Here, as we saw, this happens quickly and completely. And that explains everything! The one single organism awoke. It awoke and grew—I can't think of another word for it—and grew an antidote. Grew it the way we pick up the right tool, the right weapon to break out of the chambers. And it liberated the others."

"That means there was no madman." The captain sighed in relief.

"Don't get happy yet. There is only one conclusion."

"You sure? Maybe it's in its nature."

"That fast and that consciously? Anton, let's face it. We may be dealing with intelligence."

"Intelligence." The captain looked down at his clenched fists. "I can't drum it into my head. We couldn't have been that monstrously wrong."

"Yes we could. 'Hurry, hurry, we'll figure things out later. All there is here is animals, everything is simple, why waste time?' That's how I acted, Anton. And the robots don't give the victims a chance to react. A quick leap, a shot of tranquilizer, and they're captured."

"But there are no signs of civilization on Bissera!"

"True, there are no cities, or machines, or roads. But why would creatures that can change their bodies into machines, equipment, and materials as they need them want to build these things?"

"Impossible, Ev. Living matter is incapable of giving a developed civilization everything it needs."

"Really? As if jet engines, medicines, radar and energy cells didn't exist in nature until we invented them? Can you imagine what living matter can do if it is directed by intelligence? That impossible and ridiculous civilization from our point of view may actually be much more advanced than our own. I couldn't get out from under the glass bell, and neither could you. Not because I'm stupid, but because I am nothing without a machine, instruments, and control panels. And they always have all that with them. By the way, they ran tests on Peter while he was asleep. They could have poisoned us while we weren't taking them seriously. Why are you shaking your head? Does the idea of a madman seem much pleasanter now?"

"I'd prefer it to what you're saying now. Their behavior on this ship, at least, doesn't seem to be particularly rational."

"Our actions weren't exactly bristling with wisdom, either."

"Interplanetary war on a starship, that's all we need. Let's run a test to see if they are intelligent."

However, the test did nothing. All the routine techniques of ways to enter into contact were useless; their theoretical 100 percent certainty evaporated in the ship's silent expanses. The tension mounted. Everyone was troubled by the same question. Don't they understand, or don't they want to understand? What did their behavior mean? Perhaps Peter's meeting with the "ghost" had been accidental. But did they visit him when he was asleep by accident? Why? To take a blood sample? Or to test man's edibility? And what did his slippers have to do with it? And the locked door? It just didn't make any sense.

And why were they hiding?

It was quieter on the ship than it had ever been. No footsteps, no voices, the silence of no-man's-land that could explode into battle at any second. Time dragged on, taking any hope of a peaceful settlement with it.

A crisis occurred in the evening. The screens, which the captain and the biologist were still manning, went on the blink, one after another. One by one they went out, like candles in the wind.

The moment they had all feared and waited for had come.

Head in hands, the captain stared unblinking at the screen. He knew the orders they were waiting for. The order to attack with disintegrators, to smear the escapees all over the walls, no matter where they were hiding. Before it was too late. While there was still time. But was there time?

But the captain was also sure that earth, and his crew, and he himself could never forgive a slaughter, if Ev was correct about the intelligence of their opponents. When it was all over, when the terrifying uncertainty was behind them, people would come to their senses. The fear would be forgotten, replaced by contrition and bitterness, because the destruction of the unknown creatures would also be the end of man's certainty that he was capable of understanding everything that he came in contact with. The certainty that until now had been justified and had given men courage in the stellar worlds. And his belief in his humanity would perish, too.

The captain was as desperate, and his despair was about to turn into fury against Ev and all the theoreticians who were supposed to foresee and turned out to be blind, who were supposed to find a way out and led them to a dead end. His fury prompted him to give the order finally, because he knew that in a dangerous situation even a bad decision is better than inaction. His finger touched the intercom button.

"Wait!" Ev shouted. "I think I've got it figured out!"

"Hurry up!"

"We have to release the rest of the animals!"

"What?"

"Listen, they began the match, right?"

"So?" His finger was still on the button.

"And how did we respond? With a roundup. And they responded by making us plug our noses. What did we do? Set up traps. What did they do?"

"What are you getting at?"

"That every step we took was a direct and serious danger for them. And every answering step of theirs was more of a threat than a real danger. Our enemy isn't from the bowels of hell, it's only our lack of understanding and fear that have turned him into that."

"I'd be happier if these weren't just theories."

"They're not! Our strategy for making contact was based on the wrong premises, yet mutual understanding is still possible. We were trying to communicate with them on the level of mental abstractions, scientific concepts, in a situation when from their point of view we are the enemy from the bowels of hell. We have to deal with the root, the root of the problem! There is one basic fact that holds for all living things. Evil for any form of life is anything that hinders or threatens its existence; good is anything that promotes it. It's that way everywhere, under every sun. It's as obvious as two times two, because otherwise, if the opposite were true, life would be dooming itself to destruction. No civilization can change the criteria for good and evil without suffering for it. So we still have a chance, not a big one, but we must try. So decide."

The captain thought.

"Will you do it yourself?" His voice was unsteady.

"Yes."

"You may not come back."

"I started this mess."

The muscles in the back of his neck were stiff with tension, but Ev did not turn around. He sensed eyes on him all the time, even in places where nothing bigger than a mouse could possibly hide itself.

He was using all his willpower to walk slowly.

He walked along familiar catwalks that now seemed strange and endless. Actually, he wasn't walking, he was balancing on a fragile bridge of hopes and unfounded assumptions, which could collapse at any second. Well, he wasn't the first man to test the strength of his theories this way.

After the third or fourth intersection he had to stop, because a hole gaped in the wall. So that was how they avoided the traps. The thought of all the important wires and connections in those walls made Ev shudder. There was a pile of metal dust on the floor. Ev stood on tiptoe and looked in. What he saw was frightening. Not a single pipeline was harmed, but they were all carefully exposed, like blood vessels and sinews on an operating table.

"And we thought that we could crush them at any second, like flies. But why, why did they allow me to see this?

"Because it doesn't change anything," Ev answered his own question. "Because our very first attempt to seal this hole will be paralyzed—they'll intercept the homeostatic circuits and engine."

It was better not to think about that.

He saw two other holes in the walls, before he got to the massive door of the vitalization chamber. He rolled it back and without wasting a second began reviving the pseudosnakes. While he was manipulating the apparatus to recreate Bissera's atmosphere in the room, he kept thinking that the door he had left open would shut behind him.

And when he was finished, when the animals had slipped into the dark corners, hiding, he wanted to lean back against the wall and close his eyes.

But he had more to do. Remove the traps. A final friendly gesture. Would they take it as a capitulation?

Ev glanced over at the released animals. Something was breathing heavily behind the hood. The rest were sitting quietly as though they weren't there. The pumps, bringing in another planet's air, hissed rhythmically. The poor creatures, paralyzed by fear, the lower creatures of an alien planet. And how had it been for the higher creatures, the intelligent ones? Something monstrous descended on them down there, where they felt themselves completely safe, minding their own business, and anticipating no trouble—just that there was a horrible shadow falling from the sky at the very last moment. Then horror, darkness, and waking up who knew where, in an alien, hostile world.

Of course, their first actions were senseless, Ev thought, shutting the door. Well, maybe they were senseless only from our point of view. They maintained reason, at any rate. That means that all is not lost. For them . . . and maybe for us.

He cut his thoughts short. There was no proof that they had construed his action correctly.

None? But he was still alive! Would he have had so much self-control in the same situation, or would he have given in to the temptation to do away with the enemy?

A civilization diametrically opposed to our own. Turned inward. A world shut tight from us, for we can't understand how it is possible to create everything that we need from our own bodies, and they, obviously, can't imagine living any other way.

Say what you will, there was no single standard in the universe.

There were seven traps left. Five. Two. None.

Ev came back, enervated, still followed by the invisible eyes. Nothing had changed.

No, it had. The holes that he had passed still gaped—all except the last. It was closed so neatly that the spot was recognizable only by the shine of new metal.

Making a huge U-turn in space, the starship headed back to Bissera.

# *Nothing but Ice*

We were on our way to blow up a star.

Romantics and adventure lovers need not read any further. There's nothing here to ignite the imagination. Here is the basic plan. The flight there and back takes forty years. Plus another year or two for the Project. With anabiosis, we could sleep for nine-tenths of the time, so that we could return to earth still fairly young. But science, art, and life itself would have made such significant strides during our absence that we would inevitably return completely out of things.

But that was all right. Nothing to it. We would spend our remaining days peacefully and quietly, basking in our glory. Very long last days. Why do you think Amundsen in his declining years suddenly rushed to look for Nobile, a man he had no particular use for? Because he was an active man who had tasted a full measure of victory and risk and could not face a long, respected, and colorless old age.

Well, perhaps you think that exciting events, or unusual research, or adventure awaited us in outer space, giving us a chance to prove our courage? No way. Our job required technicians, not heroes. Just very diligent and careful workers who had no business taking risks or any independent action. Otherwise we would not be able to complete the Project.

You, of course, understand why I capitalize the word.You know that starships, however contradictory this may sound, cannot be used for interstellar travel. At medium speeds, of say 200,000 kilometers per second, a flight to the nearest stars would take decades. Speeds approaching the speed of light make it possible to reach the other edge of the galaxy. But Einstein's paradox comes into effect here: a year on board ship becomes equal to centuries of earth time. And that makes the whole idea ridiculous. In both cases, man is relegated to hanging around the sun, while myriads of seductive but unreachable worlds beckon all around.

Implementing and realizing the Project would open the door to other galaxies. According to theory, a momentary release of energy, commensurate with that of a star, would create a time-space tunnel that could be used by a spaceship, without endangering the crew and without any paradoxical consequences.

But it all had to be tested. Not on earth, naturally, and not near the solar system, which might be destroyed by such an experiment. And we didn't have the technology to tow the annihilators to a safe distance. There was only one way: to blow up a star with lasers and see what happened.

Not just any star would do. Besides, within the parameters of our capabilities, there was only one star that fitted all the qualifications. And that's where we headed.

I'm sure that the fantastic descriptions of interstellar travel in the science fiction of the last century made many a heart skip a beat. I really don't want my account to be a wet blanket, but the truth is the truth: there is nothing duller than space flight.

Judge for yourself. You will have noticed that traveling along a familiar rut makes the days blend into a gray blur. After all, it's the things that stand out from the everyday that you remember, and it doesn't matter where they happen—at home or in a spaceship.

Except that everything in a starship is much more monotonous, because unexpected things show up on screen much less frequently than they do in your apartment window, and there's no way for chance encounters or new faces to appear on board. So the months spent out of anabiosis are extremely dull.

I suppose a writer or a psychologist would find plenty to interest him. For example, the mad passion for games which came over even Timmerman, the creator of the Project theory, who would never deign to stoop to such nonsense back on earth. But almost everyone had developed his own harmless quirks. To my surprise, I became interested in numismatics, having discovered that even the mental collecting of ancient brass, silver, and gold coins was inexpressibly attractive. And since there were no books on numismatics aboard, do you know what I used to do? You won't believe this, because I barely do: I used to look for references to coins in the novels and encyclopedias we did have, catching every reference to their appearance, size, and depiction on head and tail. I had never suspected what music there is in the words "tetradrachma with an Athenian owl" or "Constantin's ruble."

But I'm getting off the track. It's time to tell you about our only adventure, which doesn't resemble an adventure in the least—except for the element of unexpectedness.

The star toward which we were traveling was so unimportant that until then it had merely been catalogued with a number. Before takeoff someone had suggested naming it, but the proposition had been rejected, though no one could come up with a good reason why not. I think there was an ancient superstition at work here. It seemed pointless to give it some neutral name, but to call it Hope or something like that . . . no, it was better to leave things the way they were.

But everything develops according to its own laws, and since no normal man is going to repeat a long series of numbers dozens of times a day, the star finally became called Nameless.

We had a lot of work to do within its system. We had to put the laser generators into orbit around the star; stabilize and tune the measuring equipment; gather all kinds of preliminary data; and finally—at the very last second—set off the robot scouting ship, which would slip down the time-space tunnel. And there were hundreds of other things to do.

Among them was exploring the planets of Nameless. There were only four of them. Two gaseous giants like Jupiter aroused little interest, since we couldn't land on them. The closest one, a small, bare planet, was about as exciting as a mound of dross. And the last one was even worse—an iceberg of frozen gases, just a useless icicle stuck on to the edge of the solar system.

But it seemed more interesting than the constant view of the unblinking stars and the ship's quarters, as familiar as the palm of my hand. We were all eager to participate in the exploration of the doomed planets, and I was lucky enough to be picked for the scouting party.

We landed—and were stunned.

We were in a blue-white world, surrounded by cliffs with mirrored, silvery crystal towers, promontories, portals, filigree vaults, rotundas, galleries, and columns. It was Gothic and Rococo, the Taj Mahal and Kizhi, everything that had ever been created by the genius of architecture and everything that it could possibly create in the future.

Ice shapes are expressive anyway, but on this planet the force of gravity was lower than on earth and the material was more complex and varied. The arches seemed to be flying; you simply could not imagine them immobile, because a single moment of rest would bring them down in a heap. A vast vault would be supported by glass columns, and in the shadows of the hanging cornices you might come across a Notre Dame. The cornices reminded me of butterflies about to take flight; their frosty design showed double in the slender plates of translucent ice.

But that wasn't all that made the landscape unique. The sky over the planet was generally murky. But once in a while it cleared up, and then—we never did figure out the reasons—the star changed dramatically in the sky.

Its light began to shatter, like water coming from a hose suppressed by a thumb. The rays fell, creating rainbows. Sparks flew from the cracks, crevasses, and slopes. The reflections, refracted hundreds of times, filled the air with dancing light. Our eyes, used to dull colors, could barely stand it.

The ice became flowing and light-bearing. Chains of miraculous constructions went up and transformed themselves within it. Spectral cities, which shone, grew, became monuments, faded, changed, and revived, were everywhere, engulfed in rainbows. It was an art form of the fourth, fifth, or some other wild, magical dimension.

For hours we made no measurements, took no notes; we were simply incapable of doing anything. We were in the thrall of a feeling more sensitive and profound than mere rapture or joy. Naturally, they could see everything from the starship, but for the first time in the history of stellar expeditions, not one of them reminded us of our responsibilities.

Then, when we returned, it all went as though nothing had happened. As though there had been nothing!

Sometimes I envy those who lived in earlier times. They could behave with such spontaneity. "The blood rushed to his head, and he unsheathed his sword . . ." Of course, things weren't that simple back then either, but at least decisions revolved around a piece of bread, the satisfaction of desires, and the defense of personal safety, and there was a code of reactions developed over generations that served man in a variety of situations, since life itself didn't change that rapidly. Then life became more complex, and the reactions became more complex too. Man was forced to repress his elemental reactions, because in the new, complicated circumstances, they only made things worse.

We had all been disturbed by the planet, as never before, and we faced a tragic decision. But what good would an outburst have done? It would have led to conflict, and arguments on board ship are more dangerous than fires. Everything had to be thought out calmly, quietly, alone, taking all the consequences into consideration. We had plenty of time. That's how we had been trained—it was the only way on starships, where the whole group depended on the actions of the individual. In a sense, we were a single brain. Therefore, I won't describe the personal emotions of the expedition members—who was silent, who was grumpy, who tried to smile. All this is secondary compared to the unpleasant duty that faced us.

In blowing up the star, we would destroy the planet. With our own hands, we would have to destroy nature's masterpiece, unequaled anywhere.

It was comparable to depriving oneself of the colors of the sunset. We were going to rob mankind, which didn't even know what it would be missing.

Was the Project worth it?

The Project would hand us the keys to space. In destroying one beautiful planet, we would get millions of others in return. No more doubts!

That was true, but nature did not repeat herself. We would never again find the beauty that would perish.

On the other hand, what was that planet? It was beautiful, and it was boundless joy to see it. But, after all, it was only ice, nothing but ice, while the benefits of the Project were real. And let our feelings rebel as much as they want!

But whether or not we conquered the galaxy, our material interest would not suffer. That meant that the Project served only to satisfy our intellectual curiosity, nothing more. And because of that we had to destroy the planet? Because we considered one desire more valuable than another?

But which was more valuable? If we hadn't mastered the space around us by the beginning of the twenty-first century, then industry would still be crowded on earth's surface. And that would cause it to overheat. Expansion into space was necessary for life. And the same kind of necessity, even if I couldn't grasp it, was motivating us now.

It was all logical. But if we were given the choice of losing our lunar stations or our moonlit nights, which would we choose?

That's how I spent my sleepless night.

Who needs a magical, wondrous planet, if you have to spend a lifetime getting there?

It was like a fresh breeze in my cabin, when I found the decisive argument.

Decisive? With the Project, distances like that would be nothing. And then the question would be: at what cost was it achieved?

It was easy to imagine what people would think then. Why couldn't we merely return and report on the new circumstances? They would find some other way; maybe we would expand into the galaxy a hundred years later, but we would do it! And without paying such a price.

Why did we have to decide on our own?

Because . . .

It was a horrible thought, and I chased it away. Of course, it came back. Who had the greatest interest in realizing the Project? We did. Because we had devoted our lives to it. Didn't this motive outweigh the other considerations?

People wouldn't say it, but they would think it. And they would be right.

And objectively? All right, beauty has no value, and theoretically it can be sacrificed. Practical people had done it right and left for ages. In the past. And then came the time to pay for it. For the poisoned rivers, the razed forests, the denuded landscapes. We inherited a bitter lesson, and we swore: never again, no matter what the circumstances!

Never? No matter what the circumstances? Extremism is always a mistake. The galaxy, with its millions of planets and stars, is an outlet for human energy, it's a salvation from stagnancy, it's limitless development. In its opening vistas we will find undreamed-of things. Amazing worlds, unimaginable life forms, the wisdom of other civilizations. So should we turn around and leave, so that it would happen a hundred years later?

Big deal, a hundred years.

That's right. If someone had put off the appearance of the steam engine by a hundred years, where would we be now?

There was no decision that could please everybody.

We understood each other so well that it was clear to us without discussion that it had all been thought over and that no one had found a way out. And it was time to make the decision, because we were wearing ourselves out.

In the good old days, people had an out. The leader would say yes and the rest joined in, soothing their consciences by saying that the leader knew better. There was no one to lay the blame on for us—those were the norms of our times.

The psychologist began the discussion. For some reason he suggested we look at the stereo videotape of what we had seen on the planet.

No one disagreed, and many felt a surge of hope. He had to have a good reason. Maybe he'd found a way out.

Our lunch lay untouched before us. The spectral cities arose and disappeared before our eyes, and a miracle of color took place before us, infinitely moving, filling us with joy and rapture. The tape didn't convey everything, and yet . . . A jangling spoon grated on our nerves.

The last frame flickered, and for a few moments we couldn't decide which was more real—the room with the table and the food or the grandeur we had just seen.

The psychologist's voice brought us out of the reverie.

"I must disillusion you. My suggestion is not a way out, but . . . press a button, and the tapes are gone, as though they had never existed. And I can wipe your memory clean of the planet, too. And where there is no memory, there is no pain, right? We will complete the Project, the world will never know what it lost, and no one will suffer from guilt! Shall I erase?"

Silence. Then:

"No! We'll remember it all. Don't wipe it out!"

It was the first time I saw the faces of friends in anguish. For all I said about emotion, nature is nature.

But the shouting died down, the psychologist spread his hands in embarrassment, and we all reverted to our usual selves.

Then, coolly and calmly, at least on the surface, we decided. You know what the decision was.

# The Snows of Olympus

FIFTEEN MILES of the rise were behind them, in the bluish haze, in the orange shimmer of the dawn, and the rest disappeared in a broad sweep toward the sky.

Vukolov and Omrin had been looking at the rise for a long time, only the rise, ascending upward, stubbornly, and apparently not getting any closer to their goal. The gloomy path pushed monotonously against the sky with its aloof, shining stars. It was only when they halted at the crest that they saw the astonishing vastness below. The eye fell into infinity, confusedly seeking familiar proportions and scale only to have the mind correct its mistakes. For what seemed like a blanket of night fog from here was actually the entire thickness of the atmosphere, and what looked like a ridge of cliffs was a mighty mountain range. And the entire expanse of the dawn was compressed into a colored piece of yarn thrust into the darkness.

It was cloud-quiet. Their blood rang thinly in their ears, and their eyes, now accustomed, ranged over the abyss, their bodies felt weightless, and only the solidity of the rock beneath them reminded them of the crude corporeality of the world.

The men sat transfixed.

"The Short Happy Life of Francis Macomber," Vukolov whispered, following the free flow of his thoughts.

"The Short Happy Life of Francis Macomber," echoed Omrin.

And silence descended once more, eternal in a place where there can be no wind. The minutes passed and the two men sat immobile.

What did they mean? What train of thought had led them to an old tale by Hemingway? What did they have in common with Macomber? They couldn't have explained it themselves.

Vukolov kept returning to his past, which from this vantage point seemed distant, small, and unreal, like a landscape seen through the wrong end of binoculars. A boy with flaxen hair raising clouds of warm dust with his bare feet—was that really him? Was that long-haired teenager arguing until he was hoarse with other excited young people in a smoke-filled room also him? Or that well-dressed, energetic young scholar at the lectern? Strange . . . And that black night when he learned that his beloved didn't love him and that it was all hopeless—did it happen? Could this moment above the abyss of abysses be a continuation of his past?

It was, and Vukolov marveled at the twists of life that had brought him here. It was almost programmed, preordained that he had run around barefoot, and that as a child he had shown great scientific ability, and that he had suffered from unrequited love, and even that he was on Mars. Why not, after all? Of course, out of billions of people only hundreds got to Mars, but they were sent there by the will of humanity, as inexorable as the force that kept the planets in their orbits. But there was no pattern—at least, no logical pattern—in the train of events that had landed him here on the mountain. Actually, it had happened contrary to all logical expectations and common sense. There was no obvious reason that forced them to scramble up this mountain. A petrographic survey of the crest? Yes, perhaps. But to tell the truth, that was merely an excuse. He had simply been carried away by Omrin's arguments. He simply wanted to master the mountain, and he permitted himself to be convinced that it was necessary for science. A whim, a caprice, and nothing more. And here he was.

What madness, if you thought about it! One century passed after another and people didn't even think about going up into the mountains. Of course, they did go up, and a lot, but only to create a path, or reach a pasture, or lead a caravan, or hide from attack. All clear, self-evident, everyday needs. People were interested in mountain passes, in slopes rich in ores, and in peaks that were good for reconnaissance, but not in just being close to the sky. Why climb for no reason? When Petrarch decided to climb up to the top of some dinky hill in the foothills of the Alps, which anybody could manage, but which no one in the memory of the locals had ever tried, he was embarrassed. He was afraid of being mocked, and he distrusted his own whim. No one climbed mountains for the hell of it. And he had. Was it God or the Devil who had prompted him?

Mountain climbing is the product of leisure. So be it. There were people who had time in the past, and the ancient Greeks had it, but there is no written record of Socrates, Plato, or Aristotle feeling the urge to climb Mt. Olympus. Or of any of their contemporaries climbing Mt. Olympus. Later on, yes: after the gods had died.

And it really took off in the nineteenth century. Dozens, hundreds, then thousands and millions of mountain climbers. A movement that dwarfed even the great migration of nations. It was a sport, yes, and a proving ground, and a school of courage. But wasn't that a justification after the fact for an irrational passion? Mountains had maimed and killed so many people. It was a rather dubious way of achieving health and building character. And so what? So as a rule mountain climbing had no practical use, no real goal, we don't care, we'll climb anyway!

And he climbed. On earth. And now here on Mars. Just like that, for the hell of it.

Marvelous irrationality.

The allotted rest period was ending. Omrin and Vukolov got up, silently turned their backs on the abyss, and moved up the slope with a steady, short stride.

Vukolov went on reluctantly. He would have liked to tarry for just an hour. But upward and onward, no matter what . . . it had happened so many times in his life.

They were on the third day of the ascent. Far below the dawn's light was so bright that it outlined the cliffs. In contrast, the sky seemed even blacker, casting a funereal shadow on the slope. The murky path among the drifts was gloomy. No imagination could have come up with anything drearier than stone fields under black sky, and when the sun's weak light cast their shadows, Vukolov shuddered at the sight of them moving so clumsily yet aping all their movements. The souls of the departed might move that way in the land of the dead, and the landscape there would look like this.

Crunch, crunch, crunch . . . their boots crushed the black pumice slag. The sound wasn't transmitted through the air, of which there was almost none, but traveled along their spacesuits and their bones.

There had been no difficulties to complain of yet. The mountain did not present serious problems and did not require great mastery of the art. They had been wise to spend so much time studying the stereo pictures of the mountain as they plotted their course. This route made the mountain resemble a greatly magnified Mt. Elbrus, without its ice caps, snows, and meteorological vagaries. Day after day, hour after hour, the solid slope went on. On earth such a long climb would have incapacitated a man in the first few miles, but here the men, the suits, and the equipment weighed much less. And there were no problems with breathing, because they had a steady supply of oxygen. Nevertheless, the endless slope tired them, and the body went into an automatic, indifferent stride soon after they resumed the climb.

Crunch, crunch, crunch . . .

Or the silence when they stepped in the soft sand, gray like everything else here.

Gravity, which they were fighting, pressed on their shoulders, exhausting them. Of course, things were working just the opposite in reality: every mile lightened them. But it felt as though they were breaking through a thick solid mass. Their hearts, lungs, and every muscle cell were working at maximum power, the way they do in a deep-sea diver. Only here the tension lasted for long hours and endless miles. The body begged for descent, but the will, merciless, forced it upward.

Now Vukolov's entire existence was concentrated on the slope, where nothing came easy and there could be no short cuts.

The sun rose, the shadows thickened, looking like the ones on the moon, and the sky turned slate and starless. Mica and quartz sparkles blazed in the angular rocks.

A half-mile from the top their path was blocked by overhanging cliffs. Either making a frontal approach or circling them would take too long. But there was a way through them. And while the river of stones that squeezed between the cliffs was undoubtedly scree, it didn't seem dangerous—they had come across rock debris on many a trip. They stepped carefully onto the unsteady accumulation.

At first everything went as planned. The small pebbles lay inert under their feet, and in the sunlit crevice they could make out the source of the scree, when the stone flow suddenly shifted and began moving down. The trembling lasted only a second or two, their hearts resumed beating, and it was over. They had lost ground, but that was the only damage.

A new, and extremely careful, attempt to move up resulted in the same threatening displacement.

Having waited for the movement to stop, they headed for a cliff, where logic suggested that the debris would be less treacherous.

It trembled even more.

A step to the side and then back to get out of the scree, then to the side and back again. But it was useless. As in a dream, silently, pebbles began jumping overhead, and a stone struck Omrin's leg. They met with a rumble that threatened an avalanche wherever they tried.

This would not have frightened them on earth. There was no gaping abyss behind them, just a sloping incline, down which they could slide with the scree if it came to that. With their experience, they would get away with a few bruises and scratches.

But they couldn't take that risk here, because a tear in their suits was much more dangerous than a broken limb. What used to be an advantage had quickly turned into a liability, proving once more that in the mountains, as in life, nothing comes easily.

With uncertain gestures, like blind men, they groped and tested and came to the conclusion that their only hope, strangely enough, was in scrambling up the axis of the flow. It displaced the scree but didn't disturb its shaky equilibrium. They even retained a little of the height they gained each time. Just a trifle, inches, but it was a gain.

They hadn't exchanged a single word. They understood each other. There was nothing to discuss, and no calculations could help here; they could only trust their intuition. Nodding simultaneously, they stepped onto the undependable escalator, the stone stairway of the mountain, going down.

The sun was behind them, but the walls of the crevice reflected it from all sides. The rocks blazed with sparks. Vukolov, intuitively picking the best support, carefully placed his foot, testing slowly, and just as carefully placed his foot there again, and nevertheless slipped down, to start all over the hundredth, and maybe the thousandth time. The climate control on his suit was working perfectly, yet sweat was pouring down his face. Vukolov saw nothing but the hot reflection from the rock and the chaotic rubble at his feet; his peripheral vision also caught the sparkling overhang of the cliffs, which was the only way of gauging their progress.

Their exhausting movement was everything now—the past, the present, and the future. Nothing had existed before, nothing else could exist later. Up—down, up—down, up—down . . . Rustle and crunch, the dry sparkle of the rock, it had always been thus, he had always been here, always scrambling, eternally slipping, and climbing back up. Only once in a while he would feel regret that there were no stairs going up in the world; they all dragged you down ruthlessly, unless you scrambled against the flow. There was a mockery, an unfairness, about it, which both discouraged him and made him stubborn.

He wasn't thinking of himself or his chances; he only heard his blood pounding in his ears and his attention moved from the spot he had chosen for his foot to giving support to his comrade, who was being borne downward. Once in a while a black swatch of sky entered his field of vision. And it too was part of his exitless life, like the battle for inches, like the rustle of displaced scree.

Slipping back, Vukolov stretched up, up, up . . . and so it went forever.

And suddenly it was over and he was lying on solid rock, staring up at the sky without a thought in his head. And Omrin was lying next to him, and it was good, only his legs were still fighting the river of stones and his heart was gradually calming down. The future seemed vast and wonderful, endless unto the ages.

They reached the top in the middle of the day.

They stood on the crest, rulers of Mars. To the left there was so much space, depth, and distance that they could see the foggy curve of the planet itself. The side of the mountain, with its cliffs, scree, and abysses, fell sharply, gradually immersing itself in the transparent blue air. Through the blue they could clearly see the rusty dry peaks of other distant mountains, the wrinkled folds of the plains, set off by the dark shadows of the canyons. Closer to the edge of the planet, the air grew darker, like deeper water, and the reddish sandhills seemed like sand ripples on the ocean bottom. Washed out by the distance, they grew vaguer, so that at the edge they blended completely with the air.

And above it all, blazing in the dark sky, was the white sun, small and blinding, blurred at the edges—a weak hint of the corona, which was invisible now.

To the right there was another abyss, enveloped to the very bottom in the shadow of a gigantic crater's funnel. From a distance of dozens of miles they could clearly see the brown, gray, and purple stones on the far side of the rim, the smallest of which could actually crown any peak on earth.

Vukolov felt that he was bathed in crystal cascades of light, cosmic light, in a place where everything was cosmic, as on the first day of the universe. The air in his suit hadn't changed, but he breathed easily, freely, deliciously, and his blood pulsed vigorously through every cell in his body. And the stony sleep of the planet only excited the boiling life within him. Who says that man is not immortal, not invulnerable to ennui, old age, despair? Who? Vukolov felt he had enough strength to last for centuries, and joy coursed and bubbled within him.

"Nix Olympica," he muttered blissfully. " 'The Snows of Olympus.' So that's what you're like."

Glowing, he turned to Omrin.

Omrin stood very still. His usually mournful face, now expressionless, was turned to something above Vukolov's head.

"Hey!" Vukolov shouted at the top of his lungs. "We took it! We took it after all!"

Omrin shook himself, as if from sleep, and looked uncomprehendingly at Vukolov. And then his expression brightened.

"You can also add that we're the first," he said with strange mockery.

Vukolov smiled merrily, like a child.

"That goes without saying and is not of great consequence!" He tossed back his head.

"What is then?"

"Everything. Everything!"

"Let's sit down," Omrin suggested.

Vukolov sat down readily and quickly jumped up, paced, and sat down again.

"Some peak, eh?" said Omrin. "A special peak. A helicopter can't come here—there's no air. Not enough space for a rocket. You need legs to get up here."

"Naturally," Vukolov said, lost in thought. "That's the beauty of it!"

"What is?"

"You know the answer yourself. What spaciousness!" He made an expansive gesture around him. "I feel like singing and laughing. I can feel wings sprouting. Only there's no snow. 'The snows of Olympus.' Without snow. Poor planning, huh? Well, I don't mind. Don't you feel like flying? I feel that I could just soar. Totally irrational. 'The joy of battle cry and standing on a cliff so high.' Why? I don't know and I don't care."

"And I came up here for the answer."

"Boring pedant." Vukolov laughed. "I'm tired of answers. We spend our lives looking for answers, that's all we do. Why don't you look around you instead of thinking? What a mountain! And yet there's nothing special about it. I mean, so it's high, so it's far. The air below us, the planet at our feet. But I can't tear myself away from it. It's all at the limit, beyond the limit—and I can reach out and touch the sky."

"So here we are," said Omrin seriously, even with a sigh. "We climb up and we feel happiness, intoxication, we even want to sing hymns. But happiness isn't just handed out like that, it's always a reward. But for what, in this case?"

Omrin's tone made Vukolov wary.

"What are you leading up to?" he asked unwillingly. Omrin was ruining his mood.

"You don't see anything . . . unusual here?"

"Unusual?"

Vukolov looked around in confusion. And once more, but differently now, he was amazed by the wild power of nature. He even felt redundant here. Everything was excessive. All the people in the world could have gone into the crater, fitted in there, and not a jot of the landscape would have been changed by it. Perhaps there would have been a little gray spot at the bottom. And even if there were air on Mars, the cry of millions would die out before reaching the crater's rim.

"There's nothing unusual here," Vukolov said, lowering his voice. "And everything is unusual. Really! This mountain could be a throne for God or Satan, but luckily, we're no longer children. We've climbed the highest peak in the solar system accessible to us, that's all. Be happy, man!"

"We did it by risking everything!" Omrin replied. "Did you ask yourself for what?"

Vukolov shrugged as much as his space suit allowed and leaned back against the cliff.

"Well, so we did," he replied. "So?"

"We have to figure it out. Two main needs determine the behavior of all living things. The need for food is one, and the need to propagate the species is the other. Did either one have anything to do with our act?"

"Why this primer on the theory of psychogenesis?" Vukolov frowned. "You really picked a good time and place for it. All right, all right, I'll answer. No, they didn't. Are you satisfied? Or shall I remind you that besides these two basic needs—"

"—there are others. Those who live without social ties are doomed to cold and death. Thus a third basic need—the striving to be with your own kind. And it's clear that it had nothing to do with our climb. There's only one basic need left. The one without which experimentation and experience, and therefore adaptation, are impossible."

"There you go! Let's congratulate ourselves on being brought here by a passion for knowledge, and let's drop the self-analysis. The mountains await us!"

Omrin snorted.

"Do you really believe what you're saying? The passion for knowledge . . . You can examine and count every grain of sand on this planet from a satellite, but what can you see from here? The satellites have lab stations. What do we have? What analysis can't they do from up there? What observations require the presence of man up here?"

"All right, all right," Vukolov grumbled, saddened by the unnecessary argument. "I agree that our action was meaningless. Or, for justification, it's atavism: the need to touch everything with one's own hands. Even gloved hands. So what? If it's a whim, it's a whim. Man does not live by knowledge alone. And there's no need to seek a deep-seated cause. It's marvelous up here without one."

"But you do want to know the cause, don't you?"

"Get off my back! Just look around. We're the first ones to see this! What silence in it all—the cosmic sleep of a planet. The mountain ridges at our feet are like the spines of ancient monsters. Time has feasted on them—look, only their bare bones remain. No, I can't express it in words. We need a painter, a poet! And you keep harping on your analysis. What, why, how . . . there's no problem here."

"There is a problem," Omrin replied, standing. "And it gives you no rest, either, friend. A whim that people risk their lives for? A caprice that gives such satisfaction? Nonsense! Nature is calculating: happiness, just like sorrow, serves the goals of survival, and all you have to do is dig around to discover the need that has been lost in the course of evolution."

"A fifth basic need—losing your head and climbing mountains?" Vukolov laughed, no longer hiding his irritation. "What a shame that science knows only four! What a coup if we can prove the existence of a fifth." And he thought: another minute and I'll tell him to go to hell.

"That's what I came up here for, for proof."

Vukolov looked up in surprise at his friend. He didn't recognize quiet Omrin. He seemed bigger, he had expanded to fill up space, and the dark, impassioned, unrecognizable face of a prophet looked down at Vukolov. "Amazing," thought Vukolov. "Is that the man I roomed with for so many months! What happened, how? Can you ever know someone else?"

"There is a fifth basic and powerful need," Omrin intoned, his words ringing like copper bells. "It exists, and I didn't expect to find proof like this here, and yet I came with the dream. . . ."

Omrin took a breath. Vukolov watched him in amazement.

"Listen! A tree grows as long as its roots hold, a fish tries to fill the oceans with its eggs, man greedily eyes the inaccessible parts of the galaxies. Everything strives for the limit and then beyond it. A tree's growth often exceeds the strength of its roots, fish die spawning upstream, man kills himself with self-imposed overwork. He sacrifices himself, stupidly disregarding the instinct for self-preservation! And why, why did evolution, which ruthlessly cuts out the superfluous, why did it permit this waste, why didn't it soften and regulate this drive? Because it's rational and beneficial for the species! Small efforts yield small gains. And when you're on the edge of a sword—and life balances on a sword!—then you lose. Oh no!

Total concentration and total effort are the only way to guarantee that life will flourish. And that's when we receive bliss—for giving our all, for giving beyond it. Everything yearns to determine itself, to realize its function, and that's what creates the unquenchable, bizarre, and even ruthless urge of life! Those are the rules of the game: you can't sit around with your arms folded. That's a law! And breaking it brings boredom at best, making the world a dreary place. And mountain climbing is just a local, private expression of this drive, but an eloquent one. Going beyond the limits in a pure form, so to speak. There!"

Vukolov was impressed, feeling both admiration and disbelief. But the innate skeptic in him took over.

"Very interesting!" he said sincerely. And then added cautiously: "But I think there are more exceptions than rules here."

"Of course!" Omrin was pleased for some reason. "The need to propagate the species isn't natural to everyone, either. But it's a rule. A single homogeneous mass is inert and inflexible, but conditions change! Today one thing is important, tomorrow another one will be uppermost, and among millions there has to be variety. Otherwise . . ."

Omrin made the gesture used by Romans to send gladiators to their death.

"Phew!" Vukolov sighed noisily, trying to shake off an uneasiness. A new image of the man he had known for a long time worried him, the way everything he didn't understand did. "It's an elegant hypothesis, but a dubious one. You were saying something about proof. Here?"

"Absolutely."

"Well . . . I don't see it. Phobos has risen on the horizon—that I can see. Such a sweet, opal crescent." Vukolov was fumbling around for the right tone to take with him. "The shadow in the crater has moved—now there's something yellow glowing in there, sulfur, I guess. But there's no life here. And can't be. Unless you mean us? But there's no other proof. You were just joking, right?"

"Wrong!" Omrin laughed triumphantly. The prophet in him

disappeared. " 'The snows of Olympus.' We're not the first ones. There was life here before us."

"Where?"

"Look around for it just as I did."

Vukolov was infected by his excitement. He stood up. His wary gaze ran from peak to peak, peering into blinding crevices and black abysses, but he only saw sunlit chaos, a majestic panorama of cliffs, rock that had been dead from its volcanic birth, totally and forever. A terrible and beautiful inertness emanated from everything, for even in the worst storms, when the air of Mars was thick with sand, the peak of Nix Olympica reigned calmly over the whirling sands.

"There's nothing here."

"You're looking in the wrong place," Omrin said gently. "Wrong place, wrong way."

"How then?"

"The mind sees before the eye does. There are thousands of unconquered mountains on Mars, but we were drawn to the highest one. Why? Because it's the highest! But if the need to realize ourselves brought us here, then it could have brought others. Can you imagine other rational creatures missing at least one of the basic needs?"

"But listen!"

"No, you answer me."

"All right. In the infinite universe—"

"Leave infinity out of this! The laws of nature hold for the entire galaxy. Rational creatures might eat stone instead of bread, breathe fire instead of air, and be composed of crystal instead of protein, but they have to eat, multiply, live in a society, study their world, and strive for the impossible. That means that if someone sometime during the existence of Nix Olympica had crossed interstellar distances, and had the time, he might have wanted to climb the highest—what other?—peak in the solar system."

"What a wild supposition!"

"We, however, are here. And we took along a laser cutter to leave our mark, not only to cut steps. By the way, the highest point of the cliff would be the spot for our signatures, right?"

"Right," Vukolov agreed.

"Then go over to that outcropping and look at what's above your head."

Vukolov took several steps on suddenly wobbly legs, looked, and blinked, as if seeing an explosion. But the shocked darkness of his consciousness was still illuminated by the writing cut into the rock long before man ever climbed his first mountain.

# *On a Dusty Path*

A small red bird spins
In all directions—have we all seen it?
—Olesha

First he heard the steps, coming closer, heavy, hollow: clump, clump, clump, like hammering on the ground. The violet bushes beyond the bend crackled, and the sirills appeared on the path. Seeing the man, they froze. They were immediately enveloped in a thick cloud of dust. The air was filled with the breathing of armored lungs.

Arkhipov felt for his gun. He wasn't frightened, but he was caught by surprise. This didn't happen in real life—the sudden steps, the unexpected appearance of monsters. It was too much like a bad movie.

They stood facing each other for a second, the man in the space suit and the animals. Then three square faces lowered, three pairs of eyes burned green, and the sirills took off like bats out of hell. Straight down the path, straight at the man. Arkhipov shrugged. A blinding flash hit the first animal. The plasma stream took off its skull.

The remaining two made a sharp U-turn. The bushes beyond the bend rustled again, and the path was clear. The swirling dust was the only reminder of the attack.

Arkhipov's knees felt weak: he finally had grasped that this was for real. Wow! he thought. This is really something to tell the guys!

He was sure that his story would interest them. Once the regulation on behavior when confronted with dangerous animals had headed the rule book. But it was soon moved back to the end. It wasn't needed. Even the most primitive animal brain could figure out that there was no point in starting up a fight with an unknown, unpredictable creature. It was simpler to wait for your usual prey.

And Arkhipov couldn't remember the regulation right off the bat anyway. Aha, it went something like this: "Avoid getting close if possible. . . . In case of attack, defend yourself quickly and decisively. . . ." Then there was some fine print in a footnote. Well, it was all in order: he had been attacked, he had defended himself, he had obeyed the rules.

He approached the destroyed animal. It had seemed bigger when it was coming at him. The dust had settled thickly on its hard shell, covering up its color. Now Arkhipov couldn't even imagine why he had thought it was dangerous. It was just a bulky carcass of bones, muscles, and nerves, which he had deprived of life. Something like regret stirred in his soul. Had it really been a predator?

Of course it was, it was attacking me, Arkhipov thought, trying to console himself. But he no longer had his earlier confidence. He was beginning to realize how unfamiliar and strange the fauna of this planet were to him. He was always in the helicopter or the buggy, almost never on foot. His vehicle would race by and he would catch something out of the corner of his eye—an animal of some kind. That's all the contact he had. What animal? Who cared! He had plenty of work to do.

His ruminations were interrupted by a rustling sound. The bushes were moving again, filled with hidden movement. Arkhipov turned his head in confusion. But the robot puttering at his feet like a dog did not emit a warning signal. So it was just some small animal making its way through the brush—a secret, invisible life seeking something, moving something, running somewhere under cover of the virgin forest.

Arkhipov took a deep breath and let go of his gun handle. An amazing thought had hit him. This was the first time, the very first time, just a few minutes ago, that he had encountered a wild animal! Could it really be the first? Yes, damm it. And the funny part was that he knew more about the animals on this planet than the ones on earth. Once in early childhood he had been taken to the zoo, he thought. But he didn't remember anything about it. And then, then? He tried to remember. That wasn't it . . . no, not that one either; he had seen that in a movie, and the other one too. He remembered! They had braked the car that had been racing down an asphalt river at 120 miles an hour to laugh merrily at the sight of the quaint leaps and bounds some little animal was making. The animal was called a rabbit, he thought. It was fascinating and so funny! It was a good thing one of his friends in the car had had sharp vision or they would have missed the sight. They had been fascinated by it. Seeing an animal in the wild! There weren't many who could boast of that. However, the earth was so combed and tamed by technology that the rabbit probably had been numbered and accounted for. It couldn't really be called wild.

All right, there was nothing so strange about it. He was an astronaut. The long trips illuminated by unblinking stars naturally separated him from earth. At least, from its wild inhabitants. "We're children of the streets, we're city boys," went the words to an ancient song. And he was an astronaut as well.

Arkhipov poked the body with his toe. He left a dusty print on the carcass. Well, this really was an exotic adventure. He could understand those people of long ago called hunters.

And then his robot buzzed in warning. Its antenna, analyzing smells, swiveled rapidly. Arkhipov listened closely. There was movement all around. Secret movement. But not a single branch stirred. The animals obviously knew how to hide themselves. What if one of them jumped out from the bushes? Should he fire in there now? Phew, he was getting jumpy, if he was thinking like that. No, gentle strolls in the woods were not for him. He wasn't used to it. He had to get back to the vehicle as fast as possible.

But he didn't have time to get back. The steps resounded again, coming closer. And the bushes beyond the bend stirred again, and as before the sirills appeared in a cloud of smoke. But this time they didn't stop, not even for a second. They rushed as though the man weren't in front of them, like a rumbling avalanche sweeping everything in its path.

Arkhipov was almost frightened by it. But he had no time to think. The gun's ray shot through the curtain of dust. The animal on the end flipped through the air and exploded. However, inexplicably and therefore terrifyingly, the shot didn't stop the attack. In the wink of an eye the sirills crushed the barrier created by their fallen brother, and Arkhipov saw their faces close to his. He saw armored battering rams, full of untamable, intense, and furious strength, battering rams aimed at him.

Again and again the ray flashed, sure, devastating, but hurried. Noise, crashes, and darkness caused by the raised dust.

And suddenly, it was quiet, because it was over. The smashed avalanche lay at the man's feet. Arkhipov didn't understand at first the strange flowers sprinkled on his space suit. Then he understood: they were blood.

He was shaking from head to toe and couldn't stop. He took a step and reeled. No, he had had enough, he had to get away from this terrible place.

But it wasn't that simple. The bushes beyond the bend weren't just rustling: they fell like a curtain, toppled by a new avalanche of sirills. Arkhipov splashed across the path with his ray gun. The first row fell, but the trembling mass hardly slowed down the animals. Arkhipov shot left and right, cutting across in broad strokes, using the ray gun like a sword. Mounds piled up before him, and he went on shooting, hitting the living and the dead; and the sirills, and perhaps more than just the sirills, kept coming, rushing him. It was a nightmare. As though nature itself had moved against the alien man to crush and destroy him.

And Arkhipov went on shooting, even though there was nothing left to shoot. The animal flood was over. When the man realized this, he had to sit down, exhausted. The overheated gun burned his gloved hand. His clothing was drenched with sweat.

But a crash in the bushes made him jump up again. What was this? He looked around, thinking wild thoughts. He couldn't tell where the crashing was coming from, and it didn't sound like the last attack. There was danger and victory in it, like the crunch of jaws devouring prey. But Arkhipov was wasting his time trying to see what was making the noise. The dust. It hung over the battlefield in a thick layer.

The rusty daylight barely broke through the dust, falling on the path in blazing patches. Their movement caught his attention. There was a strange redness in them. And motion.

"What does it mean? The animals, the light, the noise . . . I wish it would stop for a minute so that I could think straight."

The smoky dust layer trembled, as though hit by a gust of wind. The patch of light broadened and fell on a distant bush. And the bush burst into flames! Arkhipov cried out: the bush was burning with a deafening crackle.

And Arkhipov understood, immediately and finally. He understood and moaned. It was a forest fire coming at him, a fire from which everything had to flee—man and beast. It was the forest fire that was chasing the sirills down the path, the reason why they ran blindly down the most direct route, where a man found himself, so removed from forest life that he understood nothing, didn't get out of the way, didn't run side by side with the animals, but unthinkingly slaughtered them with his blazing sword, as though there was a danger greater than the forest fire.

Despite the horror of his discovery, Arkhipov felt unspeakable bitter shame. Such slaughter! Blowing animals to bits, the animals that were seeking salvation and were showing him the way to it.

Arkhipov took a last look at the sad monument to his highhandedness—the mounds of bodies now licked by flames. And he ran, tossing away his heavy gun. He ran headlong down the most direct, straight line without looking, without thinking, ready to knock down any barriers with his chest. He ran the way the sirills had run.

# The Painter

He was finally in luck: after circling the swamp for a long time, he noticed an untouched bend in the river. The pterocar, its wings fluttering like a butterfly's, landed on a grassy field. The strong current of air moved the purple flame of the cypresses. A tiny bird shot out of the pines in panic. "Whit, whit, whit," it called, its hiccupping voice disappearing in the woods.

Still not believing his luck, Gleb explored the promontory. The swamp's sinkholes formed a dotted-line boundary along one side. Fish frolicked in the river. There were no funereal ashes left by campfire sites, no footprints on the blindingly white sand of the riverbank. Signs of spring flooding—clumps of dried grasses—waved in the brush like signal flags. Gleb hooted with pleasure. The tourists had somehow missed this spot! His dream had come true. He was where he wanted to be.

Days passed, filled with the rustle of grass, the calm motion of clouds, the warmth of the sun. Maybe the whole thing was a whim. Painting untouched nature, of which there was almost nothing left—what for? There was Shishkin, Levitan, a host of other artists for whom this had not been exotic—what could he say that they hadn't?

The idea had ripened slowly and painfully, like a tree that sends its roots deep into the soil before it flings out a thick crown. His predecessors had looked upon nature with different eyes. For them, a river bend like this was a permanent staple of their art. But for him it was a brief moment in a disappearing landscape. That was his upper hand—he looked at nature, which once had reigned over the face of this earth, with alien eyes. He was an inhabitant of a country of rockets and clever machines. He knew the landscapes of the moon, Venus, and Mars. And he was a guest, for whom everything was strange and new, in a place where the painters of the past were the hosts. A guest in a dwelling that was about to be razed and that deserved a final farewell.

But a guest does not immediately sense the meaning and relationship with the host's things. Gleb perceived that difficulty right away.

Like a spaceship that makes ever-decreasing circles over a strange planet in order to land as precisely as possible, Gleb, sensing the recalcitrance of the environment, had been approaching this painting for years, getting closer to the heart of the theme with each trip.

His main problem lay in appreciating the passing landscape with the host's intuition and yet maintaining the freshness of the curious passerby. The first order of business was to find untouched pockets of Russian countryside. The official preserves had let him down. Everything about them seemed authentic, but on his first day there, Gleb had come upon a ravine that was neatly fenced in with concrete to keep the rain from further eroding the soil. He couldn't work there, he was like a diver who had to reject his customary life and overcome his entrenched habits in order to reach the bottom. One wrong move would push him back to the surface.

And finding spots that did not reveal in any way the presence of man, who always changed things to suit him, was becoming harder and harder. He would leave for the summer and find that the earth was even more crowded with another forty million people born while he was away. And each addition was like floodwater, submerging one small island after another.

The painter didn't give up—he searched, he found places, he studied them, he thought about them. But he didn't take up his brushes. After all, a marksman doesn't pull the trigger when he has the bull's-eye and the sights lined up, but when he feels that the shot is right. And so Gleb waited for the inner voice to say "now."

That summer he heard it.

Without realizing it, he was trying to do everything—walking, swimming, gathering kindling—as quietly as possible, as though worried about scaring something off. For the same reason, he never turned on his meaphone, because one flick of the dial would have allowed the noisy world to intrude, the world of high-powered business and action, crackling with energy and electricity. Back in his world, a trillionth of a second meant something—the time it takes for a thermonuclear reaction, for the engines of a starship to ignite. Here the hours stood still. They revealed only one thing: the geological epoch in which man had appeared.

One morning Gleb made a horrible discovery: there was a servorobot under a bush. It had kindling in its feelers.

"Scat," Gleb whispered. "I didn't summon you."

"You came here, I'm required to help you."

The robot's whiny voice was like a fingernail on a blackboard in the stillness.

"Scram."

"I'm a parkee, I'm obliged to help tourists. I'll clear branches, kill snakes, cook—"

"You will leave immediately. That's an order."

The robot moved its feelers—from its point of view the man was behaving strangely. But an order was an order, and the robot left obediently. It was quiet once more, but Gleb's ears still rang with the tormenting sound of the fingernail on the blackboard.

"If there's one thing that will get me through, it's time," the painter told himself. "There are enough untouched spots to last my lifetime. And there'll be time enough to find what I've missed, make up lost time, and correct my mistakes. I'm glad I don't have to rush."

He was right. He made sketch after sketch with a speed that amazed him. And he was beginning to see the whole picture: it just had to ripen a little longer.

Gleb rose with the sun, when the fog floated over the river and swamp; he drank smoky tea and sat down to work. He painted at noon, when the grass turned gray from the heat; in the evening, when the shadows thickened and the light gilded the greenery; in the morning he watched the colors awaken—the blue would be bright, but the reds glowed dimly, like embers.

All day long there was a constant low buzz—the steady song of the mosquitoes. The buzz was a soothing background for his work. But at night it made him gnash his teeth with anger: the bloodsuckers' mocking song kept him from sleep, since it heralded and accompanied their attack. Of course, Gleb could have flown out to get his ritter, and then nothing would have disturbed him, but he didn't want to waste a whole day and immerse himself in the noise of the city, which would drown out the forest sounds. And it would have been insincere to partake only of the pleasures of nature, avoiding its discomforts, which in the past man had battled constantly. That's why he put up with the chilling dampness of the long rainfalls and the boring solitude—all the unpleasant things that tourists avoided with the clatter of the meaphone and the services of the robots.

Nevertheless, he couldn't isolate himself from the times completely. At night, when the fuzzy reflections of the stars lit up in the river and he could see the map of the universe stretch out at his feet, spaceships traveling to other planets cut across the sky map. Their presence did not upset him. On the contrary, the night sky with its bright banners of the age did not let him forget that he was a contemporary painter, bidding farewell to the decline of nature the way one bids farewell to a once close person who is then forgotten. The sky was a bridge between the past and present.

The sight of the sky did depress him sometimes. Gleb couldn't understand the psychology of his ancestors, whose lives passed in the surroundings of woods and swamps. Undertaking that kind of life was too much for him. Anyone who was used to the whirlwind of business life and the variety offered by civilization and who had traveled in space would not be entranced for long by a quiet existence among the fields and sunsets. Such a man worships other gods of the heart.

A day came when the sky was high and gray from morning. As usual, the water looked threatening, frowning in weather like this, and there was no wind. Gleb valued days like this—the lighting changed very gradually, the eye didn't have to chase after quick light effects, and he could work slowly, thinking through each stroke.

He lost himself in his work. But something was bothering him. The color of the vegetation grew duller, there was a shadow creeping over it, even though everything else seemed the same. Gleb was irritated because he couldn't understand the cause of the change. He concentrated even harder, since it was the only way he knew to understand.

A cold drop fell on his hand, making him shudder. The extreme greenness of the drop proclaimed its chemical nature. How did I splash myself with chemopaint? thought Gleb, examining the drop in disbelief. Then the bushes rustled, and several drops fell on his hands, face, and clothes. All in the screaming, wild green color. Gleb jumped up.

It was pouring. Green rain. The acid-green streams fell from above and were blown from the sides, as though someone had turned on a giant shower. The chemical paint dripped down the leaves, was absorbed by the soil, and filled the air. It penetrated everywhere, and there was no escaping it. And soon the real green was covered by the artificial one like a coat of shellac.

Gleb was stunned. And he was dripping. His visual memory had forever captured the picture of chemistry triumphant over nature, over the palette of delicate shades and subtle halftones. Artifice enveloped everything, artifice visualized by a blind eye and born in the womb of a retort.

The painter dashed for his tent. There had to be an explanation for this desecration! Fortunately in his era there were no secrets and you could get an answer to any question. He turned on the meaphone.

"What's going on here?" He gave the river's coordinates.

The machine hummed for a few seconds—thousands of miles away a computer was scanning its banks of billions of bits of information for the explanation of the tiny occurrence in the valley of an insignificant river.

Finally Gleb heard a neutral voice over the noise of the shower.

"Spraying of areas that are breeding grounds for harmful insects. Being done with rainlike dispersal of a compound." The voice supplied the technical name.

"Why, why is the rain green?" shouted Gleb.

"They couldn't get the compound in a colorless form," the neutral voice replied. "They added green so that it would not interfere with the aesthetic enjoyment of the landscape during the disinfection. The compound and the camouflaging color are both completely harmless."

Gleb tossed aside the meaphone. Fools! "Aesthetic enjoyment!" For them all greens were the same.

He looked around. The rain had stopped, and the sun was out. Everything glistened with a monotonous sheen. The dead shellac had erased the chiaroscuro, equalized the shades, and turned everything into the same ugly green.

That did it. Even if the polish vanished by evening, it didn't matter. He was too late with his concept. Now he would never be rid of that sight, he would be pursued by the dead image of the artificial greenery. Everywhere, and perhaps always.

Gleb packed up quickly. There was nothing here for him now. He loaded his things in the pterocar. He looked back for a last time. The trees, grass, and bushes were all the same. Bright, bright green.

Something else was missing. Gleb didn't know what at first. Yes, the mosquito buzz was gone. The hordes of tormentors would not bother anyone anymore.

Gleb started the pterocar.

# *What Will You Become?*

THE VISITOR SPENT A LOT OF TIME scraping his feet on the mat, his glasses glimmering, unwinding an endless scarf, and finally, with a sharp "No, no, I'll do it myself!" emerging from his fur coat. Yarantsev discreetly directed his gaze toward the door, where the floor's peristalsis was swallowing up the dirty mat.

And he missed the change. A moment before it had been a bundled-up old man blustering in the foyer, and now, rumpled beard high in the air, stood a wiry, lean Don Quixote in glasses, looking boldly at Yarantsev.

"Come in," said Yarantsev, swallowing his surprise. "How can I serve you?"

The old-fashioned greeting just flew from his lips on its own.

"I'm from the studio. I'm here because of Mick."

"Has he created a ruckus?"

"Created?" The old man's eyebrows came together in reproach. "That's the wrong word. It can never have a pejorative meaning, for it is a great, important word!"

"Forgive me. What's the matter?"

"The matter is that Mick is about to commit a crime."

Yarantsev felt a chill. All his fears came alive. Always, from the day Mick was born, he had lived under the whip of anxiety.

"Go on," he said dully. "As his father, I should know everything. What crime?"

"The greatest crime that a man can commit in terms of himself. Mick is quitting the studio!"

The relief was so great and unexpected that a hoarse laugh escaped from Yarantsev's throat. The old man's mustache bristled furiously.

"Believe me, this is no laughing matter!" he cried. "If you, as his father, don't understand . . . "

"Forgive me," Yarantsev said. "I'll try to understand everything. But let's start at the beginning. So, Mick is planning to quit the studio. Too bad. I believe he's had some success over there."

"Some? Oh no. Not some—he's outstanding."

"Is that so? That comes as news to me."

And lousy news at that, thought Yarantsev. I was so afraid of alienating Mick by being too much of a disciplinarian that I became unforgivably lax. Just like most fathers, though!

"Mick is not very communicative," he continued aloud. "But I asked at the studio. The information I was given—"

"It couldn't have been anything else," the old man said, frowning. "Mick is a unique young man, and praise has to be meted out carefully."

Unique? he thought. That's for sure.

"Wait a minute," the old man demanded warily. "You say you made inquiries at the studio? When was this?"

"I don't remember exactly. . . . Apparently it wasn't you I spoke with."

"Strange, very strange! I'm not only Mick's teacher, I'm also head of the studio. I should have known. Nevertheless—"

"I should have known something about Mick's success, but, as you see, I don't," Yarantsev interrupted hurriedly. "But as far as I can see, that's not the issue. Mick is planning to quit the studio and you feel he's making a mistake."

"A huge, unforgivable mistake! He's a born thinktician."

"Really?" Yarantsev asked suspiciously.

"Apparently my name, the name of Andrei Ivanovich Polosukhin, means nothing to you," the old man said, straightening up proudly. "I don't mind. But you can ask Seding, you can ask Benkovsky—I hope you've heard of them? They'll tell you that Polosukhin knows how to evaluate talent."

"I believe you! It's just so unexpected. Mick—a born thinktician! Who would have thought it!"

Yes, that's one thing no one would have imagined, he thought to himself.

"I'll say this," the old man said, raising his forefinger. "This explanation is necessary, since thinketics is not one of your interests, and I want to have you on my side in this. Many people think of it as nothing more than a new form of art. Actually it is a synthesis, the culmination of the oldest dreams of artists. . . ."

"Yes, do go on," Yarantsev said as he began pacing the room, unable to sit still. "I'm paying attention."

But he wasn't. He knew about thinketics, and he needed to gather his thoughts. Thinketics? Well, it was a new, promising, complex art. Of course it was a synthesis. A combination of painting, sculpture, stereo film, and perhaps also playwriting and biotonics and holography. It was the direct creation of light images, without the use of hands, images that were completely incorporeal but, if necessary, indistinguishable from reality. A man sits and thinks and a complex apparatus, catching the thoughts, transforms the fantasy into colors, movements, sound, gives the mind's visions form, corporeality, false yet as real as life itself. A third form of nature? In any case it wasn't merely the synthesis of the latest technology with the oldest forms of art, but a qualitatively different level of art. There were only a few as yet who had mastered the new, difficult language. It was like the early years of film: a great new method of expressing reality, and very few creators who could breathe life into it.

And Mick was one of the hopes? Impossible, unthinkable! However, what would a talented physicist have become in an age when physics didn't exist—a wizard? Or a film director before film? Could it possibly be that nature herself designs a man for one strictly defined activity, and if there is no such spot for him in life then his fate just develops in a mad meaningless way? Just speculation; we don't know a damn thing. . . .

". . . And instead of that, your son wants to be a tamer? Do you know that?"

Yarantsev nodded. True, Mick was eager to tame wild planets. A curious situation!

"So," concluded Yarantsev, "you want me to talk Mick out of quitting."

"Precisely. I insist."

"And if the second interest is stronger than the first?"

"Impossible! It's merely restlessness and romanticism, increased by the widespread interest in cosmic distances. Creativity, the creation of objects of value by the mind and emotions—that's his true calling, not a crude attack on virgin worlds. I assure you!"

"Attack?" Yarantsev repeated. "What an unexpected association."

"Why?" the old man asked. "Struggle with the elements, important and worthy as it is, is a warlike activity—it has to be or it will fail."

"And you feel that Mick's personality is not sufficiently warlike?"

"That's not the problem!" The reply came in an irritated tone. "There are greater and lesser prospects here, and the wrong choice is a loss for society, and even worse for a man who . . ."

Yarantsev sneaked a peek at Mick's portrait. A young man's face, with high cheekbones, weathered, and not too handsome, but with a strong character, looked down from the wall. The light eyes eagerly absorbed the world; they also showed a dreamy profundity, as though their owner might be listening to an inner voice. An interesting, mobile, and not particularly exceptional face of a contemporary youth.

Contemporary? Naturally, what else?

The old man noticed Yarantsev's gaze.

"I'm not predicting laurels in art for him, but spare him a fate that is obviously wrong for him!"

"Fate . . ." Yarantsev said softly. "Do we know very much about its components? I have a question for you. If thinketics didn't exist, would Mick's talents have been as pronounced, say, in painting?"

"No." The old man shook his head. "No."

"Why not?"

"That's easier to sense than to explain. You see, painting and even sculpture are static arts. Not in the sense of expression, but . . . uh . . . if horses are running on a canvas, are you capable of picturing them beyond the canvas? Can you hear their hoofbeats in the room, feel the hot wind of the gallop on your face?"

"That's hard."

"There! But thinketics is the power to create an entire world! Not a sample, a mockup, but the world itself! It demands spatial tension, a dynamic expression of all the senses. I'm probably not being very clear—the terminology hasn't been developed yet and—"

"May I conclude that thinketics requires several personality and character traits that are not necessary at all for painting?"

"Forgive me, I'm not a psychologist. But to a certain degree . . . yes, I suppose so. But we're off on a tangent again!"

"Really? Let's be logical. You want to suppress Mick's yearning for risk and battle—a strong yearning, however temporary and fleeting it is. Let's assume that he obeys us, though I doubt if he will. What will he become then?"

"Haven't I convinced you?"

"No."

"You refuse to help me?"

"Absolutely."

The old man stared down at his hands, and those hands with the gnarled veins under the parchment skin suddenly looked like the rhizomes of a once powerful and now weakened body.

"Don't be upset," Yarantsev said softly. "If Mick leaves, there will be others, perhaps much more talented."

"All right then," the old man said, his hand coming down sharply on the table. "You do not wish to see my position, but I will fight this to the end. You of course are familiar with the 'right to talent'?"

"What's this? You're not planning to use it?"

"I certainly am!" It sounded like a battle call. "A man is free to do what he wishes with his talent if its application is not criminal and if the man is not ruining it with his behavior. In the latter case, since the loss of talent brings harm to society, society has the right to influence the individual, without resorting to violence. I'll prove that such interference in Mick's life is necessary!"

"Are you aware of the consequences?" Yarantsev was ready to explode with anger and laugh at the same time. "Society also has a responsibility: individuals who hinder the expression of talent or the development of the personality bear a great burden. That doesn't worry you?"

"No, because Mick's future is important to me." The answer was firm.

What a mess! thought Yarantsev. If I stay out of this it's possible that this fanatic will achieve his goal. Then Mick will simply fail the entrance exams—he won't suspect a thing. On his second try, or certainly on his third, they'll accept him, since such persistence indicates true interest in a profession. But should he have to go through all that? Taming planets . . . It wouldn't hurt to be sure what exactly was drawing him to that—fashion, or inherited character traits? Perhaps I should just let things go on their way? No, it's interference of the crudest type. Therefore, the attempt must be nipped in the bud. It could be done, of course, but how many people would have to be let in on the secret? It's risky. . . .

While thinking, Yarantsev observed the old man. He was frozen, as if brandishing a spear, ready to repulse an attack, ready to die in the cause. A real Don Quixote. Only the aged fingers were trembling, and the rheumy eye was on Mick's portrait, and there was such sadness in it. . . .

He loves him! Yarantsev realized. All this is due to his love for Mick, his most talented and perhaps his last pupil, the one that represents all his hopes. That's where this attempt to protect and direct him comes from! And ungrateful Mick . . . ungrateful? Mick's been so down lately. And I, blind as I am, thought it was unrequited love. And it looks like it was something altogether different. Yes, that's it. Ah, son, if you only knew yourself the way you once were . . .

"Do you have grandsons?" Yarantsev suddenly asked.

The old man sat up.

"No. Excuse me, but what does that have to do with this?"

"And you had no children either," Yarantsev continued confidently. "But it really doesn't have anything to do with what I'm about to say. Who do you think Mick is?"

"What do you mean? Mick is Mick, just as you are you, and I am me."

"Not quite. You are you, I am me, but Mick . . . A few minutes ago, talking of his future, you used the words 'warlike' and 'attack.' Coincidentally?"

"I don't understand!"

"You must," Yarantsev demanded. "Taming planets, the struggle with the elements, started a train of associations for you: attack, war . . . go on, what else comes to mind? Don't think, just answer the first thing that comes into your mind. Well?"

"Barbarians," the old man muttered. "But—"

"Names connected with it? Attack, barbarians . . . who?"

"Genghis Khan, Attila—"

"Stop! Mick is Attila."

The old man stared at Yarantsev with glassy eyes.

"That's right! Only a barbarian could treat his talent this way!"

"You misunderstand," Yarantsev said, lowering his voice. "I don't care if you think Mick is acting like a barbarian. He is a barbarian by birth. He is Attila. That 'scourge of God' that devastated Europe fifteen hundred years ago. He has Attila's brain, Attila's blood. This isn't a metaphor—he *is* Attila!"

"Very interesting," the old man said icily. "How would you like me to interpret this? Discounting these ravings—"

"I'm not raving," Yarantsev said tiredly. "Attila's grave was discovered and dug up a quarter of a century ago. A single surviving cell contains the genetic code for the entire organism. The cells were found, and the rest was a question of embryonic technology—and not very complex at that. The infant Attila was born, resurrected, created—pick one. We had no children, so we adopted him. Since Magda's death I've been bringing up Attila-Mick myself. Now he's grown. That's the whole story."

This time the words, spoken so calmly, penetrated. The old man's body shrank, contracted, his face darkened with a myriad of new lines, and his beard and mustache, whiter now, stood out and became the predominant feature of his drained face.

This lasted a minute, and then his eyes lit up again, a bright flame breaking through the ashes.

"Why Mick?"

The voice was so soft that Yarantsev didn't hear the question at first and then didn't quite understand it.

"We had to call the boy something."

"Why?"

"Why what?"

"Everything . . ."

"But that's obvious! The question of environment versus heredity. Here's the newborn Attila. And here's our society. What will become of the bloody scourge?"

"You became his father."

"Yes."

"The experiment required it."

"Of course."

"Hating Mick's past, wary of his genes, fearing manifestations of his character . . ."

Yarantsev frowned.

"The past is past," he said sharply. "Let's forget it."

The old man pulled off his glasses, as though they were seeing something they shouldn't. After a pause he asked Yarantsev without looking at him, "Mick, of course, doesn't know who he is?"

"And never will. Very few know the secret."

"Even if I tell him?"

"You won't."

"That's true too. . . . "

I'll have to be quiet about many things, the old man thought with bitter awe and pity for Yarantsev, feeling broken and helpless in the face of the blinding, unpredictable majesty of what these people whom he couldn't understand had dared to undertake.

No wonder he had sensed something profoundly personal in Mick's very first work. It was a vast plain, hopelessly green and flat, with a tiny child's figure desperately rushing toward the horizon. And anxiously and steadily, expecting the worst, the sun looked down from the sky at the child.

The old man saw the same expression in Yarantsev's eyes. The man who was Mick's father and Attila's nurturer. Who knew and lived, loved and feared, brought up a son and carried on an experiment. And who apparently couldn't understand why Mick was trying to get as far away from home as possible.

# *Things Like That Don't Happen*

In his experiments, Professor Artsinovich was as penetrating as sulfuric acid and as firm as molybdenum steel. But even steel fatigues. That day the spots were dancing before his eyes so furiously that, contrary to custom, he took his bicycle and went out for fresh air.

The countryside was not far from Academy City, and a short time later the professor found himself in an unfamiliar place. The sun shone peacefully; pines grew to the left of the dusty road, an oat field ripened to the right, and straight ahead a man was flying toward Artsinovich.

More accurately, the man was borne by the breeze, and he only made swimming motions like a frog. His rumpled pants ballooned at the knees.

The professor braked to a halt. Well, I'm really overworked, he thought. I'm seeing things.

The breeze died down and the man hung suspended a yard and a half over Artsinovich. The professor looked up at him. He felt very sorry for himself.

"Tell me, "he finally asked," do you know how to recognize a hallucination?"

"No," the man answered hoarsely, "I don't."

"Of course, of course," Artsinovich agreed. "Since you're a hallucination yourself, how could you? Unfortunately, this is out of my field of specialization, too."

"I'm not a hallucination," the man countered. "I'm Sidorov. I even have my papers."

He patted the pockets of his drooping jacket and then looked dismayed.

"I left them in my suit jacket."

Artsinov Artsinovich nodded understandingly.

"It couldn't be any other way. A visual and aural hallucination is one thing, but one that proffers its papers is something else altogether. Sheer nonsense, in fact."

"What?" the man demanded.

"Nonsense."

"Ah-hah . . ."

The man stopped in confusion.

The professor was lost in thought. He was disturbed and worried, but proud that he was behaving like a true scientist: he wasn't losing his head, or panicking, or believing in miracles. It was his own fault, there was no one to blame. He hadn't spared his strength, he had worked too hard, and something like this was bound to happen. If not this, then hypertension or, even worse, a heart attack. You could even say that he was lucky. A hallucination is not madness, just a neurosis, say. And it's easier to cure than hypertension, and painless, not like a toothache. Too bad he wasn't a psychiatrist—what a waste of material for self-observation! Well, he would do whatever he could. After all, it was his scientific duty.

"So, you don't believe in me," came a voice from above.

"Belief is not a scientific category. And I'm a scientist. And therefore I know that you are an unreal fruit of my overworked brain, alas."

"But I exist!" the flying man exclaimed pathetically. "I have children!"

"I'm not saying that you don't exist. You exist falsely."

"But I'm flying!"

"That's the point. A man can't fly on his own. That would be a miracle. People with little grounding in physics are apt to believe anything, but we know that there is no place for miracles in nature."

"I read somewhere about that . . . antigravity stuff."

"The danger of popular publications is that they spread half-truths and tend to sensationalize things," the professor said sharply. "Antigravity in this form disproves . . . you can't even imagine what it disproves."

"I can't," the man admitted. "I'm just flying around."

"There! Any manifestation of the unusual has a strict scientific explanation. That's why your case is extremely simple. Even if antigravity didn't contradict anything, where is the source of the energy that keeps you aloft? In you? Ridiculous!"

"Perhaps it was something I ate or drank at lunch. It's all chemicals now—it's quite possible."

The professor opened his mouth to contradict him, then was struck by a very simple and unpleasant thought: he was chatting with himself!

That was no man before him, it was a hallucination! And he was chatting with it.

Artsinovich looked at the flying man with hostility. The man was bobbing over him like a balloon. And he kept moving his arms, as if trying to dive. His legs were beating the air fiercely, the right foot was missing a shoe, and a toe stuck out through a hole in the sock.

"I can't get down," he said, torment in his voice. "I floated up half an hour ago and I've been up here ever since. It keeps pulling me up. My shoe fell off. Would you please help me? Hook me with something and drag me over to the pine tree."

The professor shut his eyes. The researcher must remain a researcher, yes. But say what you will, he was a specialist of a different profile. "I'll count to a hundred and then look," he declared. "The object will have to be transformed by then."

"So, I'm doomed," the voice sighed above him. "At least let my family know . . . my wife . . . in Malye Vyselke . . ."

The voice receded.

The wind touched the professor's face. "Seventy-nine, eighty, eighty-one . . ."

He opened his eyes at a hundred. The object had transformed itself all right. It was gone. There was a speck way up in the sky, a bird or something else.

Then it disappeared. The vast sky was empty.

That same evening the professor went to the hospital. The psychiatrist, with the air of a man who knew everything ahead of time, listened to him, examined him, checked his reflexes, and muttered: "You physicists, you always have to be different." His diagnosis was that the professor's nerves were shot, but that there was no great danger.

The professor took his medicine and followed his diet for a month. He was not visited by any more hallucinations.

# *A Mistake Is Impossible*

THE WINDOWS LOOKED OUT on the infinity of sky, where clouds gathered slowly and thickly, filling the hall with a soft, snowy light—a diffuse reflection of the white and blue distances. Every minute saw new cloud cities, vague and ephemeral, like a fantasy.

"Next!" called Dr. Reshetov.

The photosensors silently opened the door and a young man, still almost a boy, his face pale with anxiety, appeared in the black opening.

"Be seated!" the doctor ordered.

The young man sat in the thronelike chair, silver cords and plugs hanging from its sides.

"So what do you want to be?"

Reshetov asked the traditional question with the same good-naturedness that he had shown thousands of times.

The answer was a fluttering of eyelashes, thick dark eyelashes, a shy look from the blue eyes, a touching blush of cheeks still downy and fresh. The young man's thin fingers plucked at his sleeve.

"A poet."

"Wonderful!" Reshetov replied a little too heartily. "Your name?"

"Seryozha, Seryozha Yugov. Sergei Alexandrovich Yugov," he amended.

"Almost Alexander Sergeyevich Pushkin," the doctor joked, badly. His eyes met the young man's and he stopped short. "The card, please," he said to his assistant.

The assistant went up to the tall mosaic wall, sat at the control board in the corner, and dialed a series of numbers. The relays clicked and then a sigh seemed to run across the wall: a narrow crevice opened and a rigid yellow plastic card covered with symbols indicating Yugov's genetic code, taken in his first days of life, flew into the assistant's hand.

The young man's eyes filled with anxiety and darkened, the way the middle of a lake, secluded shyly in a glade, darkens when a storm cloud blocks the sky. Reshetov wanted to pat the boy on the back; he liked him.

But the doctor controlled the impulse. He picked up the card and brought it closer to his eyes. Usually he didn't feel the gaze of the boys and girls who sat in the chair—he was used to it. But not this time. Something had removed the veil of habit from what he was doing.

The assistant in his white lab coat—a polite and very mundane version of fate—quickly placed electrodes on Yugov's temples, neck, and throat. The boy shuddered—perhaps from the coldness of the metal, perhaps from anxiety.

Somewhere deep in the wall came a hum. The electronic guts of the computer were digesting the information flowing along the wires from the very depths of the human ego. The young man, withdrawn into himself, stared at the wall challengingly. Then he looked away.

Reshetov turned his back to him and drummed his fingers on the windowsill. He was sure the young man was staring at the back of his head.

The control light went on and the cyclops behind the wall winked its red eye: a melodic chime rang. Reshetov, without turning around, extended his hand and the cool plastic plate fell into it. He picked it up and compared it with the old card.

At their age every third one wants to be a poet, he thought. Every third one. But they usually take a refusal easily.

The thought didn't soothe him. The doctor suddenly felt tired. No, he had only thought that he was used to it. The responsibility was too great; he had to worry about the consequences. Suffering along with others thousands of times—it was difficult.

He wanted to put off the moment, but he knew that he couldn't, that there was nothing worse than uncertainty.

"Here it is, my friend," he finally said. "Unfortunately, you'll never make a poet."

He looked intently at the young man.

"Here's your card. Take it. Your abilities are marked in red on it."

He put the cold, shiny card on his lap. The pattern of curlicues—red and black—shone into his eyes. His genetic code. A tracer bullet from the future.

Nothing changed in Sergei Yugov's face. But it became older. There, thought the doctor with relief and an inexplicable disappointment. The operation is over. And now, like so many before him, he'll stuff the card into his pocket. Casually, patronizingly, he'll look at the remains of his youthful dreams. And he'll rise an adult from that chair. I don't know if there's more good or bad in it all.

The doctor had been avoiding that question for a long time, but it kept cropping up. Why? Wasn't it obvious that certainty was better than uncertainty, that knowledge was better than ignorance, and that the truth was better than self-delusion? It was obvious. He had approached this experiment inspired with the nobility of its goals; he had pictured himself as a knight of good who was given a lance by a beneficent science. Where did these doubts come from now?

The doctor frowned. Faces. He couldn't chase them out of his memory. Thousands of faces of the people who sat in that chair to test the healing power of the lance tip. Very different faces. And they all resembled one another in some way after the traditional line: "Your calling is in . . ." Some of them even shed a tear: "No, no, tell me you've made a mistake!" Others took the recommendation calmly. Still others said thanks politely and left whistling. But almost all of them agreed sooner or later. They probably agreed too easily. Perhaps because many of them secretly wished to relieve themselves of the burden of responsibility for their own fate? It would be hard to think of a better opportunity. And they left with an easy heart, headed toward the calling revealed to them by science. A calling that promised the greatest success in life for them and the greatest benefit for society. Total harmony. No need to search for yourself. And the price was cheap: the illusions (or perhaps the dreams) of childhood.

At that moment Yugov saw neither the doctor nor the room itself. He was walking amid beckoning sounds, in a quiet chapel of birches illuminated by the sun's rays, amid melodies woven by the trees and begging to be released, like a song when you feel like singing. Clouds sailed above him, strange ones, enticing the eye to follow—into the distance, into infinity. But the rumble of the bulldozer was nearby, ready to crush all this. The horizons of his future had narrowed, tracks had been laid down, black like the lines on the genetic map, and those rails went right past the sounds, melodies, and quatrains.

"No, no!" he shouted, jumping out of the chair. "You're wrong! Tell me you've made a mistake!"

He was trembling, and the blueness of his eyes dulled. The assistant rushed over to the water cooler.

Reshetov looked up in surprise. Not at the words—he had expected something along those lines—but at the way they were said. Such unfeigned pain in them.

"Calm down, son." Reshetov took him gently by the elbow. "You have marvelous talent, generous, great. But not in poetry, not in the arts. Look at the marvelous range of professions that awaits you."

He underlined the red marks on the card with his thumbnail. The young man looked obediently. Yes, they were marvelous abilities, wonderful professions, no argument there.

"But I don't want them!" The words burst out. "I want my own!"

Reshetov's face looked stern.

"You came here on your own. To learn the truth about yourself, isn't that right?"

"Yes, I believe in science! But I believe in myself, too!"

"I also believe in science, son. And that's why I don't advise disregarding its recommendations. Of course, no one's forcing you. But remember: freedom is the consciousness of necessity. And so we help you and others—if the experiment works, we help everyone to find himself and his place in the world. No one can be talented in everything, alas—that's ruled out by nature. But every man—I repeat, everyone!—has two or three above-average creative abilities in something. Everyone is talented in his own way, understand?"

"Why are you telling me all this?"

"Because all this has been known a long time. But there was no way to determine just which talent a person had. And youth searched blindly for its calling. Teachers helped, but they were working blind, too! Sometimes a person would find himself, and sometimes not, even under the best of circumstances. And he would become a failure. He would be unhappy and not know why. A happy man is not angry, but these people often became cynics, drunkards, and bums, making others unhappy too. What we're doing here has been paid for in suffering. If this experiment works out, every man and woman will know what to do on reaching maturity. And they will be insured against the suffering of the past—isn't that marvelous? You're participating in a great experiment that should sharply increase the happiness of mankind, so treat it with due responsibility."

"I know!" The young man insisted. "I know, that's why I came."

His eyes were dry now. He stood facing the window, and tiny reflections of the clouds floated in his eyes, as strange as fantasies, as bright as flames. The young man's eyes embraced the sky with the infinity of its distances and its expanse.

"Yes," said Reshetov tiredly. His soothing, professional psychologist's voice sounded hollow. "Yes, you can become a poet. At the cost of unbelievable effort and self-discipline, you can become a mediocre poet. You'll never be a good one! At least not until we know how to restructure heredity in accordance with the individual's dreams and whims. But that won't be for a long time."

The young man picked up his card from the table. He turned it around in his hand, crumpled it up, and threw it out the window. The card stubbornly opened flat, and a current of air picked it up and carried it off into the glowing blue.

"I will be a good poet!" he shouted as he rushed out the door.

"A copy will be waiting for you here!" Reshetov called after him.

And the room was filled with silence, the white and blue silence of the sky.

"Sometimes I think that this is too cruel—depriving youth of its certainty that it can do everything," the assistant said without looking at Reshetov.

"Every operation causes some pain," the doctor replied, pacing the room in thought. "But it's short-lived, the pain. And it rescues: it prevents worse future pain—from disillusionment, from self-doubt. No, we're acting humanely, very humanely."

"But some of them still shout like that. They still hope that we were wrong."

"A mistake is impossible, impossible," the doctor repeated several times.

But he was thinking about something else. Not about Yugov. He was thinking about the ones who trusted him so completely that they no longer tormented themselves with any doubts and just accepted their calling all gift-wrapped and left whistling, with confident tread, as though down a red carpet toward a predetermined future. The route was planned, and man, perhaps never having tasted love, entered into marriage with a profession. Yet, talent isn't everything, he thought. Oh, not at all—it's not enough to find it, it still has to be nurtured. Are we giving them the illusion of ease along with their cards? The illusion that they will never have to expend any effort, since the burden of the responsibility for their own futures has been taken by someone else?

"All right, the experiment is only the beginning. The future will show the results," the doctor said, dosing himself with the phrase in which all doubters had sought comfort since the dawn of time.

"Next," he called.

# *Time Bank*

THE EVENING BEFORE THE OPENING of the Time Bank we gathered in our warm family circle. The orator and oracle that night was my brother Lyova—a physicist.

"Tomorrow will go down in history," he expounded, his left eye twitching. The tic acts up whenever he gets excited.

"But I'm still worried," my wife said. She was knitting and kept dropping stitches. "I don't like things I can't understand."

"What?" Lyova demanded. "What's not to understand? It's so simple. I'll explain."

If you've ever heard a physicist trying to explain to a mere mortal the meaning of quantum mechanics or the theory of relativity, you'll understand our state. Some waves or other of time overlapping so as to create time splashes that broke off from their substratum into supratime and could be controlled—that's all that I got out of Lyova's lectures and the popular articles written by my fellow journalists. But in the long run I wasn't too upset about it. We use electricity without knowing a thing about electrodynamics, and I have yet to see anyone who was too bothered by that fact to go on living. The regulations governing the use of the Time Bank were clear to everyone. At any moment, whenever the desire hits you, you are free to pick out a bit of time and put it away on deposit. And then you can draw on it when you want to go into supratime. As easy as can be.

"You can't even imagine how wonderful this is!" Lyova continued rapturously, almost knocking over his glass. "Think how much time we lose standing in lines, waiting in restaurants, at boring lectures. Hours and days crossed out from our lives!" Despair showed in his eyes. "But no more. Now you deposit them in the bank—for the future. For example, suppose you're writing or carrying out an experiment. You're creating, you're happy. But the inexorable hands of the clock announce that you must stop and that some important responsibilities await you. Tragedy! But starting tomorrow, it will be different. You'll simply withdraw the hours you put away and go off to create in supratime."

"Perhaps we should stick to the old way?"

I gave my wife a reproachful look. You're supposed to admire progress, especially this kind.

"Impossible!" Lyova announced joyfully. "There isn't a single achievement in science that hasn't become part of our lives sooner or later. Not a single one. The coming of the new era is inevitable."

The clock struck midnight. Lyova raised his forefinger. I got up without thinking about it. The Time Bank had begun operation.

We drank a toast in majestic silence. My wife's hand was trembling. At the last stroke of the hour, our cat, which was sleeping on the couch, stretched and yawned deliciously. Poor animal! It was having ancient dreams and had no idea of the great event that had transpired.

The morning was most ordinary—gray and misty. I rushed to look out the window. Everything as usual: people hurrying, cars speeding. I gulped down breakfast and ran out into the street, followed by my wife's anxious eyes.

The bus wasn't crowded, and I took a seat good for observation. But there didn't seem to be anything to observe. I rode for five or ten minutes, and nothing happened either in the bus or outside. Sadly, I settled comfortably in the seat and took out my paper. But no sooner had I unfolded it than something pushed the paper and my arms aside, and some old man ended up in my lap!

"Sorry," he said. "You seem to be in my seat."

"Uh . . . " I muttered.

"Do you need a tranquilizer?" The old man was worried. He got off my lap. "You should have been told that I had taken off for a while."

"You . . . used it?"

"Of course. You have to conserve time at my age, you know. It's all right, stay there. I'll take this seat next to you."

The whole busload of passengers was staring at us. Luckily we had come to my stop.

I got to the office just in time for our editorial meeting and didn't have time to exchange views with friends. Strange thing about our editorial meetings. It seems as though all you have to do is sit and listen yet you get as exhausted as if you had written a lead article. It was all right while Lerovsky and Perov were talking; they went on for quite a bit, but they made sense—about the paper's coverage of the Time Bank, naturally. But then Kloponechetsky took the floor. We exchanged sour looks. And I got a brilliant idea. After all, there were many of us here and they might not notice one absence. "A half-hour deposit!" I ordered mentally, shuddering at my audacity.

It felt as though I had merely blinked. But as soon as I looked around the room I saw that I was in trouble. We were all in trouble. The editor-in-chief and Kloponechetsky were standing next to each other and their faces were lit up like a traffic signal: the editor-in-chief was red and Kloponechetsky was green. They were staring silently at the rows of empty seats.

"What the hell!"

They would have vented their anger on me alone if my colleagues hadn't started popping up in the room. Apparently telepathy does exist, since we all were seized by the same desire as soon as Kloponechetsky began speaking, and we all made our deposits at the same time.

I won't describe the tirade that followed. We were saved by the fact that the issue needed reports on the first day of the victory over time, and the office was no place to gather material. I ran out into the street fast enough to make my shoes smoke.

And I saw a tall, majestic, silver-haired citizen, looking like a monument to himself, weeping, leaning on a lamppost.

"Excuse me, can I help you?" I asked, touching his shoulder.

He stopped crying, but his voice was still uneven. "Crummy kids . . . crummy kids . . . crummy kids . . . "

A second later I had the explanation. He was a teacher. And not a plain old teacher. A master teacher, if you can use terms like that in pedagogy. And the whole class had run off from his lesson—*his* lesson!

"The kids will come back," I said, trying to comfort him.

But he was too proud and famous to be comforted. He headed straight for the police precinct. From the back he looked even more like a monument to himself.

I scribbled a note in my pad: "Master teacher. Kids. Negative aspects of the Time Bank." And went on in search of more impressions.

There was no lack of them. As I turned the corner I came eye-to-eye with a heavyset matron who was feeling around in the air and looking every which way.

"Have you seen him?" she cried.

"Who?"

"My husband!"

"What about him?"

"We were walking arm in arm!"

"But I—"

Her face became vicious.

"So! He ran off in time! Left me! Well, just wait!" She shook her fist at the emptiness and cursed him roundly. "I'll catch up!"

And she disappeared before my eyes.

Before I had had a chance to catch my breath I felt a heavy blow on my back.

"Pardon!" said a quick little man as he appeared out of thin air. "Have you noted my spouse nearby?"

"Like this?" I described a balloon with my hands. "She used it. She's chasing you."

"Aha!" The little man smiled. "I figured right."

He winked and disappeared into a nearby store. I took out my notebook, but I wasn't sure whether this should go in the positive or negative column.

I went into the nearest luncheonette, since I was hungry. The tables were almost empty and I had a glimmer of hope of a quick meal. But as everyone knows, the speed of service has nothing to do with the customer's wishes. Fifteen minutes passed after my order was taken, and I still didn't have the soup, and I was getting bored. But then I had a flash of genius. I had a half-hour saved up from Kloponechetsky's talk. I would use it to sketch out my article, and meanwhile my soup would arrive. Thanking the Time Bank in my heart, I gave the order.

My work went well. All living souls disappeared from my field of vision, since I was outside the real passage of time. No one interrupted, and the words flowed from my pen. It was great working in peace and quiet.

My half-hour was over and I emerged in reality, absolutely sure of finding a bowl of soup in it.

There was no bowl. There was no one at all.

I ran around in a panic until I found the manager, half-dead with fright. It seemed that I wasn't the only clever one. Gradually—using the same technique as I had—all the customers had disappeared, and then all the waitresses followed suit, wanting to save some time—since there was no one to wait on!

And then the radio announced that it was absolutely forbidden to use the Time Bank during working hours . . .

Angry and hungry, I rushed home. But I never did get any lunch, because that day Lyova was lying in wait for me on the landing. He was white as a sheet and steam was coming out of his nostrils.

"I was robbed!"

"Wha . . . ?"

"I was robbed! I was sitting at home and working, and the thief, moving through supratime, entered the apartment and . . ."

By evening the Time Bank was temporarily closed. They announced that they were developing new regulations for its use. They're still developing them to this day. The thief was caught, but Lyova is still mad, though for a different reason.

"They want me to make the Time Bank comfortable for everyone," he complained. "But a physical phenomenon isn't a chair—it can't conform to the shape of every rear end that sits on it!"

I don't know if he's right or not, but for many years now we've been living in the old way.

## *About the Author*

DMITRI BILENKIN is a former geologist and science reporter who is considered one of the leading Russian science fiction writers. His books include *The Surf of Mars, Smuggled Night,* and *Intelligence Test.*

## *About the Translator*

ANTONINA W. BOUIS has translated from the Russian several books and plays and many magazine and newspaper articles. Her translations in THE BEST OF SOVIET SCIENCE FICTION have been highly praised for their readability and liveliness.

## *About the Series*

In the Soviet Union, as in the U.S.A., the fascination with the possibilities of science and technology has led to a rich and long tradition of science fiction. Macmillan's BEST OF SOVIET SCIENCE FICTION is now presenting the major works in lively, readable translations, allowing the American reader to explore—for the first time—the wide range of visions of space, time, and man's future in the other major S-F tradition.